Extreme Exposure

Extreme Exposure

ALEX KINGWELL

FOREVER
YOURS

New York Boston

Copyright © 2016 by Alex Kingwell
Excerpt from next Chasing Justice book copyright © 2016 by Alex Kingwell
Cover design by Brian Lemus
Cover copyright © 2016 by Hachette Book Group, Inc.

Forever Yours
Hachette Book Group
1290 Avenue of the Americas
New York, NY 10104
hachettebookgroup.com
twitter.com/foreverromance

First edition: February 2016

Forever Yours is an imprint of Grand Central Publishing.
The Forever Yours name and logo are trademarks of Hachette Book Group, Inc.

The publisher is not responsible for websites (or their content) that are not owned by the publisher.

The Hachette Speakers Bureau provides a wide range of authors for speaking events. To find out more, go to www.hachettespeakersbureau.com or call (866) 376-6591.

ISBN 978-1-4555-6529-0 (ebook edition)
ISBN 978-1-4555-6531-3 (print on demand edition)

For Les, for cheering me on.

Extreme Exposure

CHAPTER ONE

Emily Blackstock spotted the first gunman as she was about to make coffee. It was just after five, well before sunrise. Pale moonlight washed the inky night with enough light to see across the rocky ground to the end of the long lane. A pine tree, battered by Atlantic winds, marked the entry to the road.

The man stepped out of the shadows behind the spindly tree.

Emily gave a small start. She dropped the coffee carafe onto the counter, and it fell into the sink with a loud crash.

Oh, God. Please don't let him hear.

She jerked back from the open window, thankful she hadn't turned on the kitchen light, then leaned forward to steal another look. The man gave no sign he'd heard. Tall and burly, he stood facing the old fisherman's cabin, arms held at his sides. His right arm looked several inches longer because of the gun in his hand.

Clutching her arms against her chest, the scene played out

in her mind as a nightmare she'd dreamed every night for weeks. Icy numbness spread to the pit of her stomach. How had they found her? She had been so careful, cut all connections, and even ditched her car. Used only cash. Picked a place to hide so remote it wasn't even a dot on a map.

Trusted no one.

Right now, how didn't matter. They'd found her. And they'd sent someone to kill her.

Not if I can help it.

A glance out the patio doors at the back of the cabin underlined her dismal options. The cabin sat on an island that sloped steeply to the sea. It was surrounded by rocks. No trees for cover. No neighbors. To the front was the road—and those men. To the back, the ocean. Jumping in would be sure death. Those cold, churning waves would swallow her whole.

Up front, the man beside the tree made a beckoning motion with his arm.

She squinted up the road. Two more men, barely in her sight line, climbed out of a dark sedan.

It was all she could do not to scream. Escape one man, maybe. But three? She was as good as dead.

The three men stood in a huddle at the end of the lane. Soon they would come. She couldn't just stand here. She had to try something, move.

Move!

Pulse banging in her throat, she crept around the table and chairs in the cramped dining area. She reached the patio door in seconds, paused to slip on a pair of sneakers, unlocked the sliding glass door, and opened it. She tugged at the screen door, but it refused to budge. Finally, it scraped open. Flinching at the noise, she slipped out, closed both doors. It wouldn't fool them for long, but every second counted.

Standing against the back wall, cold wind lashed her face and whipped her thin shorts against goose-bumped legs. The air smelled damp, briny. Angry waves crashed against the rocks below.

She crossed the small patio, crept down four wooden steps to the ground, then sprinted away from the cabin. Eyes trained on the ground, she jumped recklessly from one wave-washed boulder to another. It was an obstacle course of deep crevices and slippery seaweed.

Her heart beat louder and louder. It had been a mistake to think the cabin was safe. But what else could she have done? They had found her in town, almost killed her.

Tears blinding her, she ran on, landed on a large boulder. Rough rock scraped her bare arms and legs as she slid down on her backside to the rock below. Glancing back, it was too low to see the cabin or any of the men. They were coming, though, and it was getting lighter out. Her eyes darted over the rocks, seeking a place to hide. There was nothing. It would soon be daylight. They'd find her.

There was only one option. She had to get to the edge of the rocks, find a place to climb down. Try to stay out of the water. The waves would toss her back. Or sweep her out to sea.

Not daring to look behind her, she pressed on. The wind beat against her skin, stinging her, leaving a sticky film. Her lips tasted of salt. She'd never ventured this close to the water before. The rocks were too slippery, the waves too high.

Shouts behind told her she had been spotted. A second later, a sharp pop split the air.

Gasping, she dropped to the ground and crouched behind a small boulder. A bullet hit the rock. Razor-sharp fragments of granite pelted her skin like hot needles.

On her feet again, another bullet whizzed by. The last rock was in front of her. From there, it was a sheer twenty-foot drop into the roaring blackness. Blood chilled in her veins. There was no place to climb down.

Across the channel, down a ways, a man stood on the rocky cliff and looked in her direction. A small boat drifting below came into view in the gray light.

They had a fourth man, in the water and ready to go. If she went in, he would make sure she was dead.

Struggling to control her rising panic, she looked behind her. One of the men chasing her was closing in, maybe twenty steps away. The man looked at her with a steady gaze, nothing in his expression. Holding the gun at his side, he walked closer to get a better shot.

It was over. Instead of panic, she felt oddly detached, like she was floating above the rocks, watching herself. She pictured herself already dead.

Something fired in her brain. She was going to die, but she could at least delay it. No use making things easy for them.

Emily pivoted, stepped over the ledge, and plunged into the sea.

* * *

Matt Herrington stood on the mainland setting up the perfect photo. Thick, dark clouds broke at the horizon to reveal a band of red reflected in the water like fire. In fifteen minutes the sun would be up. Showtime.

Matt peered through the wide-angle lens of the camera. On the right of the frame, a small section of the island just up and across the channel protruded into the water. Black and rugged, it was a striking contrast to the water and sky.

He jerked his head back from the camera. Somebody was running on the rocks on the island. A thin, dark shape silhouetted against the flaming sky.

Right into the middle of his perfect picture.

Hairs rose on his neck. Somebody was in a heck of a hurry. Legs pumping, taking long strides. Arms outstretched for balance. It brought to mind a kid pretending to be an airplane, except this was no game.

Higher up, circles of light bounced off the rocks. Two people—no, three—chased the first person. He snapped a telephoto lens onto the camera. The one being chased was small. He scanned up the rocks, focused on the others. They were bigger. Men.

A sick feeling of dread formed in his gut. What was going on? He couldn't call for help, since there was no cell phone service. Clenching his teeth, he instinctively snapped pictures.

If the kid went into the water, his chances would be dim. The current was running fast, with big waves and treacherous whirlpools that could suck in the strongest swimmer. Dangerous even for the rowboat.

The kid reached the edge of the rocks, glanced in Matt's direction. Short hair. A boy?

The boy turned around as one of the men stepped closer to him. The man was easily twice his size. Father?

Holding his breath, Matt waited for him to offer the boy a hand. Put an end to this drama.

Big Guy reached out an arm. But not to help. He was in a shooting stance.

Fighting a wave of nausea, Matt struggled to breathe as the boy turned, stepped out over the rocks, and jumped into the water.

Big Guy walked to the edge of the rocks, leaned over, and fired into the water.

Matt felt the shock like a punch in the gut. He yelled with impotent rage as the two other men joined Big Guy at the edge of the rocks.

The men looked his way, paused a moment, as if debating their options. They backed away, disappeared up the rocks. Must have thought he was too far away to be a viable target in this wind.

For a moment, he couldn't move but in the next instant his mind cleared. Was the kid alive? Doubtful, but there was always a chance. He had to do something. Get his boat over there. Grabbing his gear, he scrambled down the craggy rock face, hiking boots finding familiar footholds. At the bottom, he untied the line tethering the boat to a boulder near the water's edge, hauled it in, and jumped aboard. The small outboard sputtered to life on the second yank of the starter rope.

Starting out across the channel, he drove the boat crosswise into the current, opened the throttle wide, and clutched the steering stick to avoid getting thrown overboard. If the kid was alive, it was a guessing game where he would surface. But it would be somewhere on the other side, maybe straight ahead if the current carried him down the channel.

The boat thumped over the waves and water slopped in, pooling in the flat bottom. The skiff lifted on a big wave and for a moment he couldn't see anything but a brightening sky. It came down and he had a clear view of the cold gray water again. The sun was up, a yellow beach ball on the horizon and the sky's vivid colors were fading into pink as night turned into day.

Agonizing minutes passed before he made it across the channel. The boat was built for stability, not speed, especially not with a three-horsepower outboard.

"Where are you?" he said through gritted teeth, his chest tightening as his eyes darted over the choppy waves. "Come on. I know you're here."

Two minutes later, he glimpsed something dark in the white froth down the channel. Riding closer, he cut the engine, half stood to get a better look. There was something there. The top of a head, the kid's dark hair.

Relief surged through him, making him light-headed. He made a wide circle with the boat, fighting waves for a half minute before he managed to pull up alongside him. Not a boy, but a girl. She stared at him, wide eyed, thick strands of short hair pasted to a pale face. Her arms flailed in the water.

Cutting the motor, he resisted the urge the dive in. If the boat drifted, they'd both be dead. Snatching a life vest, he leaned as far as he could out of the boat, his thighs digging into the wood rail. Icy water drenched the sleeves of his sweater.

"Grab the life jacket," he yelled, holding on to one end so he could drag her in.

The girl snatched a corner of the life jacket, tried to tug it away. "Leave me alone." The words came out as a moan.

"I'm trying to help you." Realizing he was scaring her even more, he modified his tone. "I'm not going to hurt you." He wanted to wrap his hands around Big Guy's meaty throat, squeeze the life out of him.

She wasn't a girl, but a woman, maybe in her midtwenties. The hair was very dark, maybe black. It was impossible to tell the exact color because it was wet. Her pale face with delicate features gave her an ethereal kind of beauty, adding to an impression she would disappear if he didn't get her out of the water soon.

A heavy wave washed over her. Gasping, she spat out a mouthful of seawater.

He reached out to her. "If you don't get in this boat, you're going to drown, or those men will get you." Big Guy and his crew would know she was alive. Maybe they would be thinking about getting a boat at the resort so they could finish the job.

The woman looked around and long seconds passed before she seemed to realize she had no choice. He could have killed her already if that had been his goal. Holding on to the life jacket, she kicked her feet as he pulled her in.

Kneeling, he grabbed the woman under her arms and dragged her into the boat. Even sopping wet, she was light as a feather, and not tall, either, five inches over five feet at the most. He plopped her down on a bench seat.

Her skin was as white as her T-shirt. She wasn't wearing a bra and the wet, translucent fabric clung to round breasts. She might as well have been naked.

Swallowing, he averted his eyes. Looking at her was a bad idea.

The woman folded her arms across her chest and leaned forward, rocking back and forth. She coughed, lifted her head, and stared at him with the greenest eyes he had ever seen. They were big and wild, the pupils just tiny black dots in the center.

Sitting down, Matt wrapped an arm around her and pulled her close. "I'm not going to hurt you."

She didn't say anything, just squirmed under his embrace. She was trembling, her body trying to warm itself. If she stopped shivering, he would worry. Even in August the Atlantic could induce hypothermia.

Rubbing her arm, his hand accidentally brushed the soft curve of a breast. His body responded with a jolt, like a hot signal firing down a wire.

Touching her was a bad idea.

Releasing her, he took off his sweater and handed it to her. She stepped over the seat and sat at the front of the boat, facing him. She had delicate features, soft lips, an upturned nose, and a small chin. But it was those luminous eyes that made him want to grab a camera.

Those eyes measured him as she pulled on the sweater. "Who are you? What were you doing on the rocks?"

"Taking photos."

She narrowed her eyes. "What kind of photographer takes pictures at night?"

"Not night, twilight. I was there for the sunrise." He turned around to start the boat's motor, glanced back at her. "I should be asking the questions. But right now we need to get the hell out of here."

She looked at him warily, as if she was still deciding whether to trust him. It didn't look like things were going his way. "Where are you taking me?" She yelled to be heard over the noise of the engine and the waves.

"My campsite, a couple of miles down the coast, on the mainland. I have clothes there, and a car."

"Why don't we just go back to where you climbed down?"

"It's farther and it'd be against the tide. Plus, it's just barrens up there. Nothing for miles around. I just stopped in to take some pictures."

The woman tightened her arms across her chest. "I can't let you get involved in this."

Matt scoffed. "What do you want me to do, throw you back in? Pretend I never saw you?"

She didn't say anything, just sat with her body rigid, staring at him. The sweater dwarfed her small, delicate frame, hanging well past her thighs, making her look vulnerable, though there was intelligence and a spark in those electric eyes that told him she was a fighter.

The eyes told him something else. Something about her looks wasn't quite right. Her eyes didn't match the dark hair. She'd done a dye job with the darkest color she could get her hands on. Her hair would naturally be much lighter, maybe blond, and the haircut was choppy, like she'd done it herself. In a big hurry. A shiver ran down his back. What the hell was she involved in?

Back on the mainland side now, halfway down the channel, they moved quickly with the current. There weren't any other boats in sight.

He decided a couple of questions couldn't wait. "I'm Matt. What's your name?"

"Emily."

"Okay, Emily, who's after you?"

She didn't say anything more for a moment, as if she was considering what to disclose. "I don't know who they are. All I know is they killed my cousin and they tried to kill me." She looked out at the water a moment before meeting his eyes again. "Now they'll kill you."

"I don't intend to get killed and I don't want you to get killed either. The more you tell me, the better off we'll be."

"Just put me ashore at the closest place you can. I can take care of myself."

He let out a snort. "Are you kidding? Those guys are serious." She was in way over her head, and either didn't know it or was too stubborn to accept help. A recipe for disaster.

"You don't think I know that?" Her eyes darkened. "I know it better than anybody. But your part in this ends as soon as you put me on shore."

Shaking his head, he said, "My part in this doesn't end until I deliver you to the nearest police station."

The look she gave him was pure terror. His heart squeezed, as if someone had reached in and twisted it. He tried for a reassuring smile, but there was a sour taste in his mouth. Scared of the police? What the hell? He had a bad feeling about this.

In the next instant that feeling went from bad to worse.

At the end of the channel, a boat appeared as a dot on the water. It could have been a sport fishing boat, of course, chartered at the island resort by a group with nothing more than striped bass on their minds.

But this wasn't a fishing boat. It was headed for them; he'd bet his life on it.

CHAPTER TWO

Cursing under his breath, Matt throttled back the engine of the row boat. The big boat was a couple of miles away, but coming fast in a straight trajectory, the dot growing like a bad stain before his eyes. Ten minutes away at most. How the heck did those guys get on the water so quickly? They must have already had a boat.

Emily's expression was grim but not surprised. "What are we going to do?"

Slamming his fist against the boat, he racked his brains for options. They couldn't outrun the bigger boat to the campground. He swore under his breath. There was no choice but to turn around, head back straight into the current. "We have to go back up the channel, try to find a spot to climb on the rocks." Even as he said it, it sounded hopeless.

Turning around, he steered the boat close to the cliff, where the current wasn't as strong. It was still slow going, not much better than treading water. This was going to be a huge clusterfuck.

A glance over his shoulder showed the boat gaining quickly. It was under a mile away, its hull bouncing up and down as it sliced through the water like a bullet toward them. It was one of those charters, with a powerful motor for offshore fishing. They didn't stand a chance. He cursed again, aloud this time.

When he turned back, Emily was standing with one foot planted on the side of the boat. His stomach clenched in alarm. "What are you doing? Sit down."

Her eyes were calm and cold. "It's me they're after. If I jump, they'll let you go."

Matt felt himself go sick deep in his gut. "No way." When she didn't sit down, he jerked the joystick so the boat swerved hard left. Emily lost her balance, toppled onto her side on the wooden seat.

Pushing herself upright with her elbow, she glared at him. He didn't care. Sure, his chances might be better alone but he wasn't about to abandon her. Who did she think he was?

Any fear he'd had was gone, replaced by a cold anger that made his heart hammer. He had to get them out of this. But how? They had to get ashore, but the only place with low rocks along this stretch of coast—where he'd come ashore earlier that morning—was too far.

The other boat was close enough to see two men, one at the wheel, another one leaning against the windshield. Big Guy.

Scanning the coastline, his eyes stopped on a dark shape at the base of the cliff a hundred feet ahead. What was it? A big wave came, and the boat rose up like a bucking bronco. More waves followed. Matt clenched his fist on the steering stick. Seconds later, the waves let up and he found the spot again. A sea cave. Water pounded the rocks, tearing into the small gash.

His mind flashed back two decades, when he and another boy had waded in at low tide. It was deep, with a small opening at the back that gave access above ground. It had been huge then, forty feet high and half as wide, but would soon be submerged at high tide.

Pointing out the cave, he said, "Right now, that's our only chance. We can get in, but the other boat is too big."

She stared at the cave, turned back to him, incredulous. "It's filling with water. We'll be trapped."

"I think we can get out the other end."

"You think?"

"There's an opening we can climb out of."

Her eyes got even bigger. She wasn't buying it. "What about the tide?"

"It'll be underwater at high tide, but we have a few minutes."

He looked away, unable to bear seeing the terror in those eyes. God help them. Their only chance wasn't a chance at all. If they managed to get out of the cave, they'd be easy targets above ground. But what choice did they have?

A noise came, a loud growl over the rumble of the waves and wind. The speedboat was right behind them. Pulse quickening, he pointed the rowboat at the mouth of the cave and rode full speed. A bullet blew a hole through the wood panel at the back of the boat, inches from where he was sitting.

"Duck!" he yelled as the boat shot through the narrow slot. Whirling, he caught a glimpse of the speedboat framed in the opening of the cave before the current sucked them into the murky darkness and out of sight.

Matt cut the engine as the dank, musty smell of the cave assaulted him. "There's a flashlight in my pack. Can you get it?" His voice bounced off the walls. Every sound amplified, the waves boomed like thunder as they smashed against the walls.

Emily found the flashlight and switched it on. Stalactites hung like icicles from the ceiling, while dark rocks jutted out from the walls.

"How far do we have to go?" Her voice was sharp and brittle as glass. The temperature had dropped a couple of degrees, and she rubbed her arms.

"Not too far." What if the hole had caved in? He gave his head a little shake. Better not to think about that. They couldn't go back.

Emily shone the light at the ceiling. As each second passed, the passage became narrower and narrower. Now, the wet, jagged walls were close enough to touch, the ceiling just a couple of feet above their heads.

A minute later, as the boat reached the far end of the cave, the flashlight picked up a gaping hole in the ceiling. It was large enough at the opening for two people, before it turned a corner and the light from the flashlight bounced off the slimy black walls. He remembered crawling on his stomach as a kid through some tight squeezes. At one point, he'd been sure they wouldn't make it out. Part of the passage was man-made, carved out decades ago for some reason that escaped him now.

She stared up the hole. "How far is it to the top?"

"Forty, fifty feet?" He pointed to a rock ledge near the edge. "We'll climb up from those rocks."

"How small is it?"

"It's small, but it's on a slope, maybe sixty degrees, so you can crawl. There's not much climbing."

Jamming the boat against the ledge, he picked up his pack, turned to Emily. She wasn't moving. Hands clamped over her mouth, she gave the impression she was screaming inside.

"What's the matter? We have to hurry. The cave's flooding."

She shifted her hands to speak. "I'm staying here."

* * *

Emily grasped the side of the boat as it bashed against the cave walls. There must have been a hole in the hull, because icy water sloshed in the bottom, soaking her sneakers and splashing against her legs.

Indifferent to this, she said, "I can't go up that hole. I will die."

Open-mouthed, he stared at her as if she were insane. "You'll die if you stay here."

The tightness in her chest had become a crushing sensation so intense every breath hurt. But worse, much worse, was the thought of going up that hole. There was no way. She'd have to burrow like an animal to get out. For who knows how long. An image of herself trapped, suffocating, flashed across her eyes.

She didn't want to die like that.

"I'm not going." Meeting his eyes, her voice came out strong. "But you have to go."

Matt sat beside her. Earlier, in the channel, she'd had the impression of a man who was dangerous, capable of violence, as if nothing could stop him from getting what he wanted. It had scared her, yet oddly had made her feel safer at the same time. Now, he was like another person, the small smile on his face transforming him into something softer, less intimidating.

He wasn't much over thirty, but there was a maturity to his hard-boned face, with the two-day stubble, prominent eyebrows, and strong jaw. Framed by longish dark hair, it was a face that said, *Trust me, I'll take care of you.*

It didn't matter what kind of face he had. It wouldn't help. A lump clogged her throat, making it hard to swallow.

Go. Leave me alone.

He said, "You can do this."

There was no trace of panic in those brown-black eyes or that deep voice. It was as if he had all the time in the world, as if the cold, murky water wasn't swooshing around their legs, rising quickly as the seconds ticked by. "We're in this together. I won't go without you."

When she didn't say anything, he added with a tight smile, "Hey, I did two tours of duty in the Middle East. If I survived that, I can survive anything. Come on." He got up, reached a hand down to her.

A hammer struck her heart. It was emotional blackmail, even if unintended. If she didn't go, they'd both die. She would be responsible for the death of a war vet. How pathetic was that? Tears stung her eyes. There was no choice. And he knew it, damn him.

A new idea surfaced, and she snatched it like a lifeline. She would climb to the high-water mark, far enough to save him. But that was it.

Wiping away tears, she forced herself to her feet, put one

hand on the side of the boat to steady herself, and grabbed his hand with the other. She wasn't sure who she hated more at that moment: him, for forcing her, or herself for being such a coward in the first place.

"You go first," he said. When she shook her head, standing her ground, he said, "It'll be better if you don't have somebody above you. You'll feel less closed in. Trust me."

Yeah, and that way you'll make sure I go.

Matt reached into his knapsack, pulled out a headband, and tied it on. It made him look rough, almost savage. "Once we start going, we'll get out fast. I'll shine the flashlight up so you can see." He grabbed the knapsack, but left his tripod in the boat.

The first part wasn't a problem. The hole wasn't straight up, but steeply pitched, and there was enough room that they could have climbed side by side. She concentrated on finding places to put her feet and hands, and then pulled herself up. Water rushing below was a reminder of the need to hurry. After several minutes, arm muscles sore, she let her legs do the work.

The wide part ended. Ahead, the chamber veered to the left and narrowed abruptly, like an upside-down funnel. Stomach churning, she stopped, called out over her shoulder, "Why don't we stay here? Wait for the tide to go out, and then we can climb back down." The boat, smashing against the rocks, was barely visible in the darkness below.

"Too risky. Those men can get in when the tide drops." Climbing up beside her, he put a hand on her shoulder. "I'll talk you through this. It's not far to the top and it's on a slope.

We should be able to crawl." He handed her the flashlight. "Push it along in front of you."

"You go first this time." She wouldn't get very far, and there wasn't enough room for him to get past her if she stopped. He had to go first.

He hesitated, seemed about to argue, then said, "Keep in mind that if I can get through, you'll have no problem. You're a lot smaller."

After a quick smile, Matt pushed his knapsack into the hole, crawled in. First his head disappeared, then his shoulders, torso, and legs. Soon just the soles of his boots were visible, before they too vanished.

Her chest tight, she pulled in a deep breath, let it out, then got down onto her hands and knees to follow him.

You can handle this. Don't panic.

After a while, the tunnel narrowing, she had to drop onto her belly and use her arms to pull herself along. It was no longer of any use trying to convince herself she could handle it. She couldn't. Her heart beat so hard she wondered if this was what a heart attack felt like. Closing her eyes, she tried to slow her breathing, but the thick, putrid smell of decaying earth filled her lungs and she opened them.

Water swirled in the chamber below them, still rising. If she didn't move on, it would soon lap at her feet. She wanted to ask how far they would have to go to be out of its reach but the effort seemed too much. The rock was wet, making it impossible to tell if the water at high tide came this far. Above her, the flashlight illuminated Matt's boots but little else.

"Keep coming." His voice was muffled but calm. "We'll get out of here."

Stifling a curse, she took shallow breaths, not daring to risk deeper ones because it would make her bigger than she already was. Progress was by inches now. The passage had shrunk so much it seemed incomprehensible he could squeeze through. She came to a corkscrew, twisting first her upper body, then the lower to get through. The rock walls were a dark, writhing monster pressing against her. Cold, slimy. A wave of nausea churned her stomach. She fought the urge to vomit.

Matt's voice broke through again, soothing, encouraging. Closing her eyes, she slithered forward, heard his voice without taking in what he was saying. Time passed—it was hard to tell how much, maybe twenty minutes, maybe an hour. When she looked up, daylight began filtering down the tunnel, like flakes of softly falling snow.

"Hurry," she called up. Every cell in her body screamed to be out of the cave. Now.

"Just a minute." His voice was a harsh whisper. "I hear something."

Her heart squeezed, as if a heavy boulder had fallen onto her chest. The flashlight slipped out of her hand, bounced off the walls as it dropped down the passage below.

"Something's moving around up there," he said, more urgent now.

Fighting for air, she didn't care. If she didn't get out, she would die. She tried to tell him, but her throat was tight and no words would come out. Her mind cut back to a familiar nightmare. She was a child, maybe two or three, locked in a dark place—there was no recollection of how she'd got there—screaming to get out.

No scream came now. She had the sensation of going under water, as if she were drowning. Her numb fingers lost their grip on the slippery rock. Beneath her, the gaping black hole was like a big mouth waiting to swallow her.

CHAPTER THREE

Emily!"

A voice drifted down through the tunnel into Emily's consciousness. She was lying down, her check pressed into the cold rock. Dark spots, black and purple, floated in front of her eyes. Shaking herself out of her daze, she lifted her head and saw someone peering down the hole, a dark head surrounded by a halo of blue light.

"Come on," the voice said, low but urgent. "We've got to get going."

It was Matt. He was reaching down to her with his right arm.

She was having trouble thinking clearly. Air couldn't enter her lungs. Where was she? A cave. Stomach cramping, she clawed at the rock with her fingers, pulled herself up. Let Matt drag her above ground.

Collapsing on her back on the hard ground, she closed her eyes against the blinding light, sucked fresh air into her lungs.

Her heart started racing anew as she remembered he had heard something when they were in the cave. Fighting dizziness, she forced herself to sit up.

"What did you hear? Is somebody around?"

He looked down at her. "Must have been an animal. I can't see anybody, and I don't think it would be too hard to spot them if they were out there."

As her eyes adjusted to the light, it wasn't hard to see what he meant. They had emerged on the tip of a barren peninsula, a vast moonscape of gray bedrock that stretched for miles. It was broken by a scattering of pine trees, all runts, and occasional patches of green and brown where low grasses and shrubs struggled to grow.

It was the middle of nowhere. They had emerged from the horror of the cave into even greater danger. They were wide-open targets now. Her heart raced, and her arms and legs began shaking. He said, "Are you okay? We should get going."

She gulped air, struggling for control. After a long moment, she was able to glance up. "I'm fine. I just need a minute."

He didn't say anything but his look seemed a good imitation of what a nasty drill sergeant might use on a slow recruit.

She said, "You go ahead."

He picked up the knapsack, got out a water bottle, and handed it to her. She grasped the bottle with two shaking hands, tilted it up to her mouth, and took a long drink. Her breathing was still too rapid, but she'd managed to get it down a bit. At least her heart didn't feel like it was going to explode.

Brushing a hand across her face, she stood, ignoring a feeling of wooziness that made her stumble. Steadying herself, she faced him squarely. "Thanks for helping me. I'd be dead if it weren't for you."

Mumbling something in reply, he put the water bottle back in a side pocket of the knapsack. Standing there, he looked as rugged and virile as the hero of an action movie, the filthy shirt and khaki headband only adding to the effect. He had everything but the weapon in his hand, the blood running down his face. A real-life Rambo, but leaner, better looking. Way better looking.

But definitely not her type. And way too much to handle right now. She was in no mood to tag along behind this guy, especially since it would put his life at further risk.

Her head clearing, she looked around, muttered a curse. It would take a day to walk out of here. The peninsula was about ten miles wide and fifteen miles long, jutting like a stubby finger out to the sea. There was open sea on two sides, and a long, narrow cove ran the length of the third. To the north, low gray hills of rock stretched down the finger and widened into forest at the end of the peninsula.

She turned back to him. "Do you know this area?"

"I've been here a few times. It's pretty simple. We have to get to the nearest town, Egerton, which is forty miles—"

She cut in, "Do people know about this cave entrance?"

"It's on all the park maps." He took the knapsack off his shoulder, pulled out a map. It showed the state park, just over three hundred square miles, with the cave entrance clearly marked. "If the guys know about this entrance, they may come.

I think we have to assume they will. We've got to move quickly—"

She put a hand on his arm to interrupt him, felt the tension in the taut muscles, quickly withdrew it. "I really appreciate what you've done for me. I wouldn't be alive if it weren't for you."

Dark eyes stared at her. "But?"

He was a big guy, standing close, but she wasn't about to let him intimidate her. She tilted her head back to meet his eyes. "We split up here."

He was about to speak but she said, resisting the urge to touch him again, "You should take the quickest route. I'll do a wide circle—"

He didn't give her a chance to finish. "Why are you so bloody stubborn?"

Her mouth fell open. "What are you talking about?"

"You refuse to accept help, even to save your own life."

Crossing her arms, she stared up at him, tried to keep her face neutral. She was trying to spare him, so why was he being such a jerk about it? He should be jumping at the chance, not acting like some hot-to-trot hero.

She said, "Our chances are better if we split up."

The muscles in his jaw clenched. "No, they're not."

Her chances wouldn't be as good, but that wasn't the point. She was fit, but not like him. She'd slow him down. They both knew it. She took a deep breath. Just put it in terms he could accept. "I've got a big target on my back, and I don't want you to be collateral damage."

"I'm not leaving you. And I'm not going to get killed, at

least not without putting up a good fight. Neither are you."

"If you get out first, you can call for help."

He scoffed.

"I'll be perfectly fine on my own." It wasn't like she had zero experience. Two years of Girl Guides counted for something, didn't they? "This isn't your decision to make. It's mine. And I say we're splitting up here." She hated the idea that he thought she was helpless almost as much as she hated dragging him into this mess.

"Where's your water? Food?"

Gritting her teeth, she said, "Okay, I need water. Give me a little bit, whatever you can spare. I can do without food."

The small smile that formed on his full lips was a surprise. So was the strange little flip-flop in her stomach.

He said, "We're in this together."

The conversation wasn't going at all like she had wanted it to. He wouldn't listen to reason. Worse, he seemed to have some kind of pull over her. Not good. Normally, she wouldn't go near a macho type like him with a ten-foot pole.

She blew out a noisy breath. "I'm not so big on togetherness."

"So I noticed." He put his hands on his hips, the smile still there, gently mocking. His upper lip was a bit bigger than the lower, with a little indentation that looked just big enough to fit a pinky finger.

He said, "I'll make you a deal."

She raised her eyebrows but didn't say anything, already knowing the way this was going to go. She was going to be stuck with him. He had her pegged as a damsel in distress and himself as the hero.

"As soon as we're out of this park and get to town, we go our separate ways. Okay?"

Huffing out a breath, she pretended to think about it for a second before nodding. It was more blackmail, but she had to have water. If he got killed, it would be his own fault. Besides, maybe her luck would change. There was always a chance those thugs thought she was already dead and weren't coming at all.

Matt was pointing to a road on the map. "We have to hike to this road. It's about fifteen miles, give or take."

The road came straight down from the north to the top of the cove, then curved as it followed the cove on the other side down to Egerton. He was pointing to the top of the cove, where the road was the closest.

She said, "Then we'll catch a ride to town?"

"That's right."

"What if those guys come?"

"If they're coming, they'll come along the road. They'll probably wait there, because the only way across the barrens is on foot. But we've got an advantage. They won't know for sure that we made it out alive." He looked at the map again. "There is another option."

She furrowed her brow. Not that she could see, unless her wannabe hero had wings and could fly.

He said, "We could hike to the cove, find a cabin to hide out in. I know there are a few in that area. The cove is closer than the road by about five miles."

"We'd still have to cross it to get to Egerton at some point. How would we do that? I'm not a very fast swimmer."

"Too cold to swim anyway, and too rough. But we could find a phone and call for help."

That would mean the police. She held up her hands. "No way."

Folding the map, he looked at her for a long moment. "We'll go for the road then, hope they think we didn't make it out of the cave. If we move quickly, we should hit it sometime this afternoon. We could be in Egerton tonight."

"That'd be great."

"Then you can be by your lonesome again." There was a tiny hint of amusement in his tone, as if he wanted to make sure she knew he'd won this round.

Shooting him a fake smile, she picked up his knapsack, shoved it into his chest. She had a sudden urge to sprint to Egerton, so she could ditch him. She was getting all kinds of weird signals about this guy—the strongest being red and pulsing like a strobe light across her brain. Lead the way, Rambo," she muttered under her breath.

* * *

The wind off the sea lashed against Emily's back as she scrambled after Matt. He had started slowly, but after a few minutes picked up the pace and they now leaped across the rocks. She shed the mud-coated sweater, tied it around her waist, and after a few minutes found her stride, synchronizing her breathing with the footfalls of her squeaky wet sneakers on the rough rock.

Half an hour later, she was breathing hard and struggling

to keep up. Still, the effort served to keep some of the terror gnawing at her stomach at bay. Each step brought them closer to safety.

Matt glanced back. He seemed to notice she was lagging because he waited for her to catch up, then slackened the pace. After a few minutes, he said, "Tell me what happened to you. If we want to get out of this, it would help if I knew what we're up against."

Emily forced a laugh. Really, was he trying to be annoying? "There is no 'we' in this," she said between gasps for air. "I thought I made that clear."

"There is until we get to Egerton. Anything could happen, so humor me."

"I don't know who they are. I already told you that."

"You must have some idea. Just start at the beginning."

She caught her breath. "A month ago, my cousin Amber died. Everybody thought it was a drug overdose, but I knew it wasn't." She was aware of a break in her voice. "She told me before she died that somebody was going to kill her."

Running the conversation through her head again, tears pricked the corners of her eyes. It was the last time she'd seen Amber alive, two days before she had died. They had met for lunch at a busy café, but Amber hadn't touched her food. Her hands had trembled as she lifted her coffee cup.

Emily would give anything to go back to that day, to realize the extent of the danger Amber had been in. To have done something. The only thing left now was to make sure her killer didn't get away with it.

He said, "Where did this happen?"

"Riverton, it's a town in upstate New York, not far from the Canadian border. It's where we're both from. She was killed in her house."

"I know Riverton. Did your cousin say who or what she was scared of?"

"She wouldn't tell me. She said it was for my own good. But something made me think the police were involved."

He raised his eyebrows. "The police?"

"I was skeptical, too. But I should have listened to her, because somebody did murder her. I might've been able to help her. She had nobody to turn to."

"She had no other family?"

"She didn't get along with her mother or sister. She'd had a few problems in the last couple of years, and they fought."

"What sort of problems?"

"Amber was in an accident about two years ago, a car accident. A woman in a car coming toward her crossed the center line and slammed right into her. The woman died. Amber survived, but she fractured her spine. She had to have surgery and, to make a long story short, she got addicted to painkillers. For a while, she was a wreck. But she managed to get off them. Things were turning around for her. She had a lot of help from my friend, Nicky, who works at a youth shelter and does a lot of addictions counseling.

"What did Amber overdose on?"

"Painkillers and alcohol. But that's why I knew she didn't kill herself."

"What do you mean?"

"The woman who caused the accident was drunk. Amber

swore off alcohol after that. Wouldn't drink a drop. Maybe if she'd overdosed on pills alone, I could see it, but the alcohol didn't make sense."

He considered this for a moment. "Did you go to the police?"

"They were convinced it was an accident. They refused to reopen the investigation. My mother told me to leave it alone. She said I was just causing more pain for my aunt."

She'd stopped by her mother's house a couple of days before she fled to use her computer, since her own had crashed. Remembering her mother's words, she felt like a hole had been pierced in her heart.

I think we all need a bit of a break from you, Emily. It will give you time to come to your senses and realize that Amber did this to herself. Instead of focusing on her, you should be focusing on us, on helping her mother get past this.

The rebuke had stung, but only a little more because her mother had chosen to deliver it in front of her mother's boyfriend. He had seemed uncomfortable, and Emily hadn't wanted to argue the point.

She said, "I tried to talk to Amber's lawyer, but he refused to speak with me, even over the phone. I went to his office, but couldn't get past his secretary." A small animal, maybe a mouse, scurried for cover as she stepped over a deep crevice in the rocks. "Amber had a new boyfriend, a cop, and he seemed to think the investigation was pretty thorough."

"Her boyfriend was a cop? You said something made you think the police were involved. Could it have been him?"

Stopping, Matt took a bottle of water out of his pack and passed it to her. Tipping the bottle back, she felt the cool liquid rinse her throat and had to stop herself from guzzling the whole bottle.

A large gull flew overhead, shrieked in anger, then swooped over the cliff and flew out toward the sea. There wasn't a cloud in the sky.

She said, "I only met Jason two times, but he didn't seem off to me. They'd been going out for only a couple of months. He told me he took a look at the police report and thought they'd covered all the bases."

"And you still had doubts?"

She handed him the water bottle. "I knew she didn't kill herself. The police seemed more interested in closing the case than anything."

"Why do you say that?"

She shrugged. "It wasn't something that was really obvious, more of a feeling. But until I know otherwise, I don't trust them."

He took a gulp of water, gave her a sharp look. "Something tells me it's not easy to win your trust."

She glared at him. "Forgive me if trusting people isn't high on my priority list. My cousin was murdered and now people are trying to kill me."

"Take it easy. I didn't mean to offend you."

Blowing out a noisy breath, she reached down to pick a few berries off a small shrub growing in a sheltered crevice. They were bitter and piney, almost inedible, but hunger gnawed at her stomach like some sort of animal was living in it so she swallowed them anyway. She motioned with a wide sweep with her hand that she was ready to start walking again.

It was true what he said, about her not trusting easily. But that was a good thing. Besides, it didn't matter what he thought. By day's end, she'd be rid of this rent-a-Rambo.

* * *

For the next two hours, Matt drove a steady pace as they scrambled over the barrens. Instinct told him their lives depended on reaching the shelter of the trees, where they would have less chance of being seen. But, aside from a few outcroppings of rocks and some thin pines, they had hours to go before the vast emptiness transitioned to light forest.

Hour by hour the sun climbed higher in the sky. Its harsh rays bled the colors out of the landscape so that everything looked bleached and brittle. Heat radiated from the rocky ground through the soles of his shoes.

Not hearing Emily behind him, he checked over his shoulder. She had stopped about thirty paces back and was bent over with her hands on her legs. Pinching his lips together, he walked back, took a water bottle from the pack, and handed it to her.

Straightening, she took a long chug, handed back the bottle. Her hair was damp and her face glowed with a thin sheen of sweat. "It's so hot."

"Unfortunately, it's going to get worse." They didn't have a lot of water, so he put the bottle back without drinking any. "And there's no wind."

"I just need a minute." Brow furrowed, she was the picture of determination, but she was breathing heavily and holding her stomach with her hand.

He wanted to reach out to her, but knew better than to try. Inhaling deeply, he pointed to a group of stubby pine trees about a quarter of a mile away. "Can you make it to the trees? We can stop there, have some more water. It's too open here."

In full daylight, her dark hair contrasted even more against her pale skin. It was almost as if she had tried for a goth look, but had forgotten the piercings and heavy makeup. The freckles on her nose wouldn't do, either. But there was a sort of girl-woman wildness about her that made his pulse quicken, as if he'd been shot full of adrenaline.

Catching him looking, she glared at him. "Let's go, then."

When they reached the trees a few minutes later, she collapsed on the ground near a stunted pine. Sitting down with his back against the trunk of another tree, he fished two apples out of the knapsack and handed her one. She held it in one hand, swatted with the other at the blackflies that had descended on them as soon as they stopped moving.

"Must be a second hatching, it's a bit late in the season." He reached into his knapsack for insect repellent and held the small container out to her. She shook her head, not looking at him. Maybe she was one of those health-conscious types, suspicious of the ingredients. "You sure? They'll eat you alive."

This earned him a heated look. "I'm sure."

Okay. Somebody was in a prickly mood. Couldn't blame

her, really. Thirst and hunger could do that to you, not to mention aching muscles. Bloody scrapes from climbing in the cave crisscrossed her arms and legs. And then there was the fact that killers were hunting her down. She looked terrified, a vein pulsing in her throat, those green eyes constantly darting over the barrens.

A blackfly landed on his neck, began feasting, its bite like tiny knives slicing into the flesh. He slapped some bug dope on his neck, arms, and legs, feeling the sting from his scratches.

Or maybe she didn't like him. Normally, he was up for a challenge, but this time he wasn't sure he wanted to be around her long enough to change her mind. He wasn't a masochist. The smart thing would be to get her to Egerton—he'd sling her over his shoulder if he had to—then run in the other direction. But was he smart enough to do the smart thing?

Standing up, he slipped on his knapsack. "Ready?"

"How far do we have to go?"

"At a rough guess, eight or nine miles."

Still sitting, she looked up, shielded her eyes with her hand. "Why the rush? Does it really matter if we get to Egerton a bit later?"

Rubbing a hand over his face, he wondered if putting her over his shoulder would happen sooner rather than later. "We have to get out of the open." He kept his voice even. "Once we get to where there are more trees, in a couple of hours, we can slow down."

Scowling, she stood up, scratching a red welt on that long,

pale neck. She was a pretty package, all right, but wrapped in barbed wire.

As they hiked farther inland and the soil deepened, the landscape started changing. The trees were taller, less emaciated, and the plants grew thicker. A small warbler, yellow with black streaks, landed on a nearby shrub. Bobbing its tail, the chubby bird flitted down to the ground, chased insects with a singular purpose.

They had walked for an hour, not talking much, when Emily said, "I've given you lots of information but I know nothing about you."

"What do you want to know?"

"You were in the military?"

"I retired from the marines four years ago. I build houses now. I'm from Maine but live in Boston. My dad lives just over the state border in Maine. I have a sister. She's a teacher."

She said, "Your mother?"

"She died when I was young."

She thought about that for a minute. "Why did you leave the marines?"

"I loved it, but not enough to do my whole life. Too much time away. But along the way I picked up an engineering degree, got interested in construction."

They walked for a few minutes without saying anything before she came up with another question. "When did you pick up photography?"

"I'm pretty new to it. My sister got me a camera last Christmas, said I needed to stop working so much."

He looked over his shoulder and smiled. "Satisfied? Think you can trust me now?"

"From what you've just given me?" She rolled her eyes. "I wouldn't count on it."

"Ask away. I'm better with questions."

She frowned. "I've learned that the hard way."

Her interest in him must have run out, because more questions didn't come. She obviously had enough distractions. He thought about what she'd told him. Something didn't fit. It didn't make sense that all those other people, including the police, were wrong. Did her cousin make up a story to cover a planned suicide?

Snatching up a blade of grass, he chewed on it and looked at her. "You were saying that the police wouldn't reopen the investigation. What happened then?"

She scowled. "More questions?"

He smiled. "Unless you have some for me."

She drew in a breath. "A few days after I went to the police, somebody attacked me. I was walking to Nicky's place after work. She was having a party. It happened a couple of blocks from her apartment. It was night, dark. Some man came out of nowhere. I don't know who he was. He had a baseball bat."

"What the hell? That's crazy."

"I'm sure he would have killed me, but a car came along and he took off." She lifted her hair off her forehead, showed him a thin pink scar a couple of inches long near the hairline. "The couple in the car took me to Nicky's and she took me to emergency. Eight stitches. Doctor said I was lucky."

She grimaced. "I didn't feel so lucky at the time."

Without thinking, he reached over to touch the scar but she flinched away from him.

Pulling back, she said, "It's okay. My hair hides it."

"What did the police say about it?"

"They thought it was a random attack."

He chewed on that for a second. It was possible. "How did you end up here?"

"I wasn't going to wait around for him to try again. I decided to take off for a while."

"Why the island?"

"I don't have much money. My mother couldn't help me out. I saw an ad for a waitress at the island resort in a travel magazine." She stopped short, as if remembering something. "They're going to be mad at me for not showing up for work today. They're really short-staffed." Her shoulders lifted in a little shrug. "Oh well, it can't be helped."

"I'd say." He gave her a quizzical look. With her life in danger, it seemed an odd thing to worry about. "Do you think you could have been followed to the resort?"

"I don't see how. I was really careful. And I didn't tell anybody where I was going. I just picked up and left."

"Somebody must have known somehow."

"I don't see how."

"You didn't tell your mom?"

"I told her I was taking a vacation and that I couldn't be reached. I didn't say where I was going, but I'm pretty sure my own mother didn't send somebody to kill me and I don't have any other immediate family."

"She was okay with you taking off?" If he tried to pull something like that, his dad would flip.

"She thought it was a good idea. Everybody was angry at me for asking questions about Amber's death. Amber's mom, that's my aunt, had some sort of breakdown. My mom and Amber's sister—her name is Celia—blamed me."

"Her sister, this Celia, she didn't think it was murder?"

"Celia said Amber was still using drugs. She said it was an overdose. I think everyone just wanted the whole thing to be over, maybe because her mom was unstable."

He turned to her, frowning. "Could you have been wrong about Amber not using drugs?"

That brought a glassy stare. "No, I wasn't wrong. Can we not talk about this for a while? I really don't feel like justifying myself to you."

He had said the wrong thing. "I'm sorry. You're right."

Taking off his knapsack, he unzipped a side pocket and handed her an energy bar as a sort of peace offering. "I don't have a lot of food, so we'll have to ration."

She tried to refuse but he put the bar in her hand, and watched her unwrap it and take a big bite.

He used the headband to wipe the sweat off his face and neck, stuffed it into the back pocket of his shorts. "Twenty more minutes, then we can stop and rest for a while. You okay with that?"

"Will we still get to Egerton tonight?"

"I think so. If we get a ride." Smiling, he pitched the knapsack higher on his back. "Had enough of me?"

She opened her mouth but the retort died on her lips. A

sound, the low hum of an engine, came across the water. Straining his eyes, there was nothing to see. Not yet. But he knew that sound.

Grabbing her hand, they sprinted to a small tree about thirty feet away.

Hunched against the tree, Emily stared into the distance. "A boat?" she said, holding her breath.

"Helicopter." His pulse raced in his throat as he peeked out from behind the fir tree. "They must want you awfully bad."

CHAPTER FOUR

The helicopter flew in along the coastline from the south, descending steadily in the cloudless sky as it neared the barrens.

"We have to move," he said to Emily, who had sat down at the base of the tree. The chance that they'd been spotted moving across the flat, open barrens was overwhelming. And if there were weapons on the chopper, it was game over. Bullets would make Swiss cheese of the tree—and of them.

"How do we know it's coming for us?" Panting, she looked at him hopefully as she brushed her arm across her forehead to wipe away the sweat.

"We don't, but that's not a chance I want to take."

The hope in her eyes died as she choked back a sob. "Where? There's nowhere to run."

Pointing to a small outcropping about eight yards ahead, he reached down to pull Emily to her feet. Her arms hung limply at her sides, suggesting she was close to exhaustion.

"It's our only chance. Come on, you can do it."

"You go. I won't make it in time." Her teary eyes pleaded with him.

His heart lurched. "Together, remember?" He ran his fingers over her cheek to wipe away a tear rolling down her face.

A flash of irritation crossed her face and she brushed his hand away. "You and your friggin' togetherness. It's going to get you killed."

"Yeah, well, that's just the kind of guy I am." He grabbed her hand, turned, and sprinted toward the outcrop. Sooner or later, she'd get the message that he wasn't going anywhere without her.

The chopper glinted like a diamond in the sun, coming in low and fast. He raced on, but Emily was slowing, and soon he was half-dragging her behind him. After a minute, she lost the grip on his hand and stumbled to the ground.

She said, "I can't go any farther."

He reached down, pulled her to her feet, and swept her up into his arms, one arm under her knees and the other around her back. She was nothing to carry, but his energy stores were running low, too. He pushed on, refused to think about not making it in time.

A quick backward glance showed the chopper had dropped to about five hundred feet. It dipped its nose as it raced over the barrens, close enough now they could hear the slap of the rotors. In a minute it would be on top of them.

They were only halfway to the outcropping. His legs screamed in pain, threatening to give out, and he couldn't get any air into his lungs. Sweat dripped into his eyes, blurring his vision.

Second by second, the helicopter's engine grew louder, filling his ears with its deep, thundering throb. A glance back revealed two people in the front bubble window and a dark figure with a rifle at an open door on the side.

Seconds later, they were under fire. He couldn't hear the bullets over the engine's roar and the blood pounding in his ears but they kicked up dirt as they peppered the ground around his feet.

Matt clutched Emily tighter to his chest, knowing his body shielded her. But that would only work when the chopper was behind them. Overhead, it would be another story. If he was to give her any chance of making it out of this alive, he had to get her behind the rocks.

Rage began to boil up in him. Those bastards. He couldn't let them kill Emily. His lungs burned, but the anger propelled him forward, forced him to put one foot in front of the other.

Agonizing moments later, they reached the outcropping. He sprinted to the far side, collapsed on the ground on top of Emily. There was a large vertical rock, fifteen feet high, with a narrow space between it and several shorter boulders. Picking Emily up, he shoved her in the space, slipped in after her, both of them upright.

The chopper buzzed overhead, kicking up a whirlwind of dust and dirt. The blades sliced the air with a *thump thump thump*. Dirt clogged his throat, filled his nostrils. Still panting, he covered his mouth, gulped, desperate for air in his starved lungs.

A minute later, the helicopter rose slightly, then banked off to the right, flew on. It was white, sleek, room for half a dozen people. Big enough for the job. He caught a glimpse of a thick red stripe running the length of the white undercarriage.

He and Emily stared at each other for a long moment. Rivulets of sweat ran down her neck, streaks of dirt on her cheeks, and damp hair clung to her forehead. Her nostrils flared as she struggled to breathe.

They had to stay where they were. The outcropping was their best cover. Even if there'd been something better, he had no energy left to move.

He watched, waited. Not ten seconds later the helicopter started a wide counterclockwise turn. His mouth went dry. Emily stared at him again, the look of a caged animal in those wide green eyes.

CHAPTER FIVE

The helicopter circled back, more slowly this time, and lower, not more than fifty feet off the ground. The knot in Matt's stomach tightened.

Would the pilot risk landing on the uneven ground? Likely not, but he might not have to. Coming in low would give the gunman way better odds.

Emily, holding herself tightly, had her eyes squeezed shut.

"We're going to make it out of here." His voice sounded a hell of a lot calmer than he felt. They were standing sideways, wedged in pretty far. Shooting from a moving vehicle was difficult, but a good part of him was still visible.

Seconds later, shattered fragments of rock rained down on them as the first bullets smashed into the boulders. It was a semiautomatic rifle, the bullets coming in bursts of four or five. Blood pounding in his ears, he put arm over Emily's head, tucked her in close to his chest.

He held his breath, knowing the angle wasn't there for a

good shot unless the chopper was overhead. The pilot must have had the same idea, because in the next instant the chopper hovered directly above them, so low its downwash kicked up dirt and gravel like a mini tornado. Any lower and the pilot would have zero visibility. He'd crash and they'd all be dead.

The attack seemed to go on for a long time. Blood pounded in his ears. Rock shards pelted his skin. His arms were on fire. The ground shook like there was an earthquake. Time stood still.

Then the roar of the engine receded and the chopper lifted up. The noise of the blades chopping the sky gradually decreased.

A minute later, sure it wasn't coming back, he stepped out of the crevice. Emily followed, coughing. Dust covered her like a thick gray blanket. Sitting down, she wiped dirt from her eyes. She looked at him. "Will they come back?"

"I doubt it."

"So we're out of danger?"

He avoided her eyes. "I didn't say that. But it was just too hard for them to get a good shot from the helicopter."

She stood up, brushed dirt and rock chips from her hair. "So will they try to land?"

"They can't on this rock. It's too risky, especially with the wind. Otherwise, believe me, we wouldn't be talking right now. But they've pinpointed our location. They'll come over land to get us."

"Well, that's just great." She lunged forward and slammed her hands against his chest. "You idiot."

He stumbled back a step. "Whoa. Take it easy. It's not my fault they found us."

"I'm not talking about that." Her fists pounded his chest. "You could have been out of here, long gone, if it wasn't for me slowing you down. I told you. You wouldn't listen."

"I can see you've recovered quite well." Holding back a grin, he snatched her hands in his. "I made my decision and I'm not regretting it."

She tried to wrench her hands away but he held fast. "You're still an idiot."

He stared into those blazing eyes, his heart hammering. Every time he looked at her, his desire increased. And she was damn good looking when she was pissed. "Didn't I tell you I liked a woman who didn't mind getting a little sweaty?"

The attempt at humor was met with a scowl. He didn't know what he wanted to do more, try to soothe her or just skip that and kiss those dirty lips. But now wasn't the time for either. Drawing a breath, he released her. "We can argue about this later. Right now, we have to figure out what to do."

She put her hands on her hips, lifted her chin. "We have to split up. It's your only chance. It's obvious you can't go to the road. They'll be waiting there. You have to go back."

"And you? What would you do?"

"I'll keep going."

He raised his eyebrows. "I can't go back. It's too far. There's no choice but to keep going."

She narrowed her eyes, cursed under her breath.

Glancing around, his eyes stopped on the blue waters of the cove, below them in the distance through the thickening scrub. It was their only option. "We have to detour to the cove, see if we can find a place to hide out."

"And then?"

"We'll get help."

The features on that beautiful face tightened.

He studied her a moment, sighed. "Okay. No police."

Relaxing slightly, she glanced toward the cove. "How far is it?"

"From here? Five miles, I think."

God, they were screwed.

He said, "We'd better get moving."

Although she was doing her best to look calm, those parched lips were trembling and that pulsating vein was doing triple time. She had guts, all right. He wasn't used to seeing it in civilians, especially not those that looked like she did. He ground his teeth at the thought of anything happening to her. Maybe he could keep her alive until Egerton, but after that?

"Wait here. I left the knapsack at the tree."

When he was back, he reached in and handed her a water bottle. It was about a quarter full. "Finish it up. You look like you need it."

Her thirst quenched, they set off again. After they'd walked thirty minutes, he said, "What will you do when you get to Egerton?"

She slapped at a blackfly on her neck. "Grab a shower. Eat."

He gave her a stern look. "I'm talking about after that. You must have some kind of a plan."

She turned on him, nostrils flaring, angry eyes piercing his. Her eyes looked darker, a forest green, and somehow even more brilliant, if that was possible. "How can I possibly have a plan? This just happened this morning."

He had said the wrong thing again. "I realize—"

"Plus, I've been shot at. I'm tired, hungry, thirsty, scared." She counted them off on her fingers, paused a second before she added the sixth. "And as if that wasn't enough, I've spent the whole day getting the third degree from you."

Eyebrows raised, he decided to let that go. She was still angry. He could understand that. But she should be thinking about developing a plan. A good one. He couldn't just drop her off in Egerton if she didn't have one. And the way he saw it, going back into hiding seemed the best option.

Giving her a few minutes to simmer down, he said, "You realize you can't go back to Riverton, at least not yet, right?"

Her mouth pinched. "I have to go back. If anything, this has shown me that it's no use trying to run away."

Putting his hand on her arm, he stopped her. "You'll risk everything."

"I know that, but they'll just find me if I try to hide."

Keeping his hold on her arm, he waited until she met his eyes. "What will you do? Dye your hair purple? Do you think that will throw them off the scent? God knows you can't cut it any shorter."

"Will you just give it up?" She shook her arm free. "Do you think I don't know now that a bit of hair dye won't make me safe? At least it was better than doing nothing. And it does make me look quite a bit different, I'll have you know."

He shook his head slowly from side to side. "That won't stop them coming after you."

She started walking again. "I can't run for the rest of my life. And I have to find out what happened to Amber. I can't let them bully me."

He threw his hands up. "Bully you? We're talking about people who are able to hire hit men. Get a helicopter. It's a bit beyond bullying."

When she turned around to face him, that stubborn lift was back in her chin. "I owe it to Amber to figure out what happened."

"How are you supposed to figure it out, especially if the police can't?"

"Can't or won't? Even if I disappear, they'll find me."

It was as if she hadn't heard him at all. She was calm again, her tone resolute. How could he possibly talk some sense into her? He had to try.

"I can help you disappear."

Stopping, she squinted at him. "What do you mean?"

"I could help you find another place to live. You'd get a new identity, start over. They'd never find you."

The look on her face was skeptical. "How?"

"I once helped a woman get away from her husband. He would have killed her if she hadn't. It's not easy, especially in the Internet age, but it can be done." He still kept in touch with the woman. She was still fine, her daughter growing up without an abusive father. Emily could have that chance, too. All she had to do was ask.

He said, "Before, you were ready to leave your family, your job?"

"For a little while, but not forever. To tell you the truth, if it were just my family and my job, I could do it. Especially now that Amber is dead."

"What about your mom?"

"We could figure out a way to see each other once in a while."

"She wouldn't mind that?"

She shrugged. "I think once in a while would suit her just fine. We're not terribly close. She's pretty well known in town, has lots of friends. And she has a boyfriend. He's a judge. They're a power couple. Besides, I might be putting her in danger just by sticking around."

Walking again, he said, "What about your job?"

"I work as a chef at my mother's hotel. It's only temporary. I did a year of law school. I'm thinking of going back. Harold, that's my mom's boyfriend, actually sparked my interest in law. I can't be a lawyer if I disappear."

With forced restraint, he said, "You can't be a lawyer if you're dead." The gutsy determination he'd earlier found so appealing was now irritating him even more. The thought of the risk she was taking sent a chill up his spine. How could he get through to her?

Turning around to see if his words had hit home, that determined look in her eyes was even stronger. Underneath it all, she was probably scared as hell, but it was as if she had made up her mind and nothing would change it.

She said, "I am not your problem, Matt, as much as you want me to be. I answered your questions, but that's all. It doesn't mean I want you to fix my problems."

"You became my problem when I fished you out of the water this morning."

"You did your duty. I thanked you for that. But what I do from here on in is my business."

"You don't trust me?"

"Maybe I do have trust issues." Her eyes darkened. "But I know I want to do this alone. That way if it doesn't work out, I only have myself to blame." She tightened her lips. "I don't want to debate this anymore. We're just wasting time."

Balling his hands into fists, he resisted the urge to grab her shoulders and shake her. She knew the risk, but it didn't matter. And she was doing anything she could to push him away. Why? It made no sense.

Unless she really was the crankiest, most stubborn person he'd ever met. Or her dislike of him was that intense.

Man, she pissed him off. He welcomed the anger, knowing if they had any chance of getting out of this alive, the anger was better than the desperate ache of his desire.

Turning around, he picked up the pace, knowing her shorter legs would have to do double time to keep up with his long strides.

First things first. It wouldn't matter if he couldn't get her to Egerton alive. When those guys found out they weren't headed for the road, what would they do? They would get a boat and head out on the cove.

They were totally screwed.

If they somehow made it to Egerton, against all odds, what then? She was reckless enough to go back to Riverton.

What about him? Could he abandon her to those murderers?

Or would he be the bigger fool and take her to Riverton? Would she even let him?

* * *

Emily could feel the tension radiate off Matt as he shot off down toward the cove. It was as if he had some sort of sixth sense that danger was ahead. There were more trees for cover now, but in some ways it was riskier because it meant the hit men would have the same advantage.

After twenty minutes, struggling to keep up, she said, "I thought you said we could slow down once we got to the trees."

He whipped his head around, glared at her. "That was before we got shot at. If we slow down now, we're dead."

"All right. All right. I was just asking." She motioned him forward with a flick of her hand.

She had to have water soon. Her tongue stuck to the roof of her mouth and her head throbbed, as if a thousand tiny hammers were pounding away at it.

Matt seemed no worse for wear. He was hypervigilant, constantly scanning the trees, as if he expected a gunman to pop out from behind one of the gnarly trunks at any moment. Every couple of minutes, he stopped and listened, head down. The only sounds were the wind and the buzzing of insects. Satisfied there was nothing, he would move on, taking big steps, landing on the balls of his feet to minimize noise.

Of course, he might have been just showing off his tracking skills, but there was one good thing about it. Being on red alert meant he wasn't peppering her with questions. He seemed almost unaware of her presence.

The muscles of his broad shoulders and back strained

against his dark green T-shirt. Khaki shorts hung low on narrow hips, which seemed to roll back a bit with every step.

Studying that movement, her stomach did a little flip. Did every man walk like that? She'd never noticed it before, although she'd never spent much time watching a man's backside.

Stop. What was she doing thinking about him like that? She didn't even like him.

When they got to the cove, she would jump in, stay underwater for a minute to wash off that smell, and the sweat and grime. Get her hands on some drinking water, concentrate on finding a way to get to Egerton. Get something to eat, although she wasn't hungry anymore. She'd get out of town as fast as she could, maybe beg a ride from some trucker. After that, she'd have to figure out how to pick up the investigation. Start with Jason Hatt. The last time she'd spoken with Amber's boyfriend, she'd had a feeling he held something back.

She had to get out of here first. Matt was leading her on a crazy zigzag route down through the trees. She wanted to ask if he was sure it was a direct route, because her sense of direction was all messed up and the cove wasn't visible through the trees, but she held her tongue. He didn't look receptive to questions right now and maybe he knew exactly what he was doing, which meant she would sound like a total idiot.

Looking down, she focused on picking her way over the uneven ground. The trees gave some shade, but it was still hot. Her feet throbbed and a blister was forming on her sockless left foot. Boss Man would object if she stopped to check her feet. He wouldn't say anything, just give her that cocky smile. She really didn't like him or that smile. It was too cocky. *He* was too cocky. She'd fallen hook, line, and sinker for a guy like that a couple of years back, a bad-boy type, confident and assertive, always quick with a smile. Too quick. He turned out to be a jerk, mean even to his mother. But she'd hung on for too long, done his bidding, even when she'd had his number.

Maybe Matt wasn't a bad boy, but her fine-tuned radar picked up a couple of blips of something. Women would come way too easily for a guy like him. That road could only lead to heartache.

Looking up, she caught him watching her in that way she'd become all too used to, as if he was assessing her. As if he knew her thoughts, had her all figured out. Knew how scared she was. Messed up.

You have no idea, buddy.

Half an hour later, she didn't think she could go on. Swallowing was impossible. Plus, the hammers in her head had now turned into sledgehammers, each in a competition with the other to see who could pound the fastest and hardest.

Looking up through the trees, her head spun crazily around. Trying to steady herself, she put her hands on her hips, looked down at the carpet of ferns, mosses, and lichens at her feet. When she looked up, her eyes caught a flash of movement at the base of a pine tree about fifty yards ahead.

Lurching forward, she grabbed Matt's arm and motioned with a shaky hand through the trees. "I saw somebody, behind that pine, the big one that looks like it has two trunks," she whispered. "Close to the ground."

"Get down." His voice low and urgent, he quieted her with a finger to his lips.

They crouched down. She listened to the soft rustle of the wind in the trees and the sharp, buzzing call of a small bird. With shaking hands, she clutched a handful of moss, squeezed it tight as she ran scenarios through her head. If it was the men, she wouldn't stand a chance. She had no energy left, but Matt could run.

After a minute, he stood up. "It's okay. It was just Mr. Fox." Amusement tinged his tone.

Letting out a breath, tears sprang from her eyes, completely unexpected. She looked down at the moss, soft and feathery in her mud-caked hands. She couldn't do this. It had been a false alarm this time, but what about the next?

"Are you all right?"

Wiping her eyes, she forced herself to her knees.

He knelt down in front of her, and his deep-set eyes examined her face with new concern. He had the beginnings of a five-o-clock shadow, the dark stubble thickening around his chin. "We're going to be okay. I'll make sure you get out of here."

Warmth crept into her cheeks. There was too much sexy in those eyes, full lips, and strong cheekbones. There were flaws, too, his eyes a little too close together, the jaw a touch too prominent. Oddly, those imperfections only made him better looking.

He reached his hand out to her shoulder, and she leaned back quickly, crossed her arms in front of her stomach. She couldn't have him touching her, pitying her. She didn't want to be this person she felt like right now, weak, unable to handle herself. Worse, she didn't like the way her body craved him. Wanted him to touch her, even though her brain tried to fight it.

Putting a hand on the ground, she pushed herself up, avoided his eyes. "Let's go."

They didn't stop until an hour later, a mile from the cove. Crumpling to the ground, she started a damage inventory. Thirst emerged the clear winner, followed by the pounding in her head and the legs like rubber bands stretched to the snapping point. Prying off her shoe, she added the blister, an inch-long raw patch on the side of her foot.

He looked at it in disgust. "Why didn't you tell me? I have a first-aid kit. We could have fixed it up."

She narrowed her eyes. "I thought we didn't have time to stop."

Letting out a huff, he said, "I think you would have been able to go faster if your foot was okay."

"That's great." Her tone was frigid. "Nice to know you're more concerned about going faster than the fact that my foot was killing me."

A shake of the head suggested he was finished with the conversation.

She would have felt better if he'd looked worse for wear. But he didn't. Sitting on his haunches, his head was straight up, the longish hair falling loosely over his face. Unfocused eyes looked into the distance. Maybe he was wondering how much of a target he was, now that they had seen him with her. Maybe thinking about what his next move would be. Whatever it was, emotion didn't come into it.

He stood up. "I'm going down to the shore to scout around, see if any of the cottages are empty. I'll see if I can get some water."

Grabbing her shoe, she said, "I'll go with you."

"No, wait here." He pulled a small first-aid kit out of the knapsack and handed it to her. "See what you can do with your foot."

She put on the shoe. "I'm okay."

"No, you're not. Your face is beet red. You need to cover that blister. I'll be back as soon as I can." He handed her a folding knife from his pocket. "If anybody comes near you, use it. The blade's not very long, but it's sharp as hell."

Swearing under her breath, she glared at him. Who did he think he was, acting like a drill sergeant? He'd saved her life, sure, but that didn't mean he could boss her around, treat her like some boot camp recruit.

He said, "If you get a chance, don't worry about aiming for anything, just hit whatever you can and keep hitting."

"I can't do that."

"You have to."

Swallowing, she said, "Do you make a habit of this?"

"Of what?"

"Bossing people around? Playing the white knight?"

Hands on his hips, his dark eyes pierced hers. "I don't think anybody can be your white knight."

She scowled. "You obviously think I'm a damsel in distress. I have to sit and wait under a tree while you go on your little mission."

"Why are you trying to make something out of this that

isn't there?" His voice was a whip. "I'm just trying to save my own skin. If those men are down there, they'll spot two people faster than one."

He waited a second for her to say something, but when she didn't, he turned around, picked up the knapsack. Gritting her teeth, she watched him slip away into the trees. He didn't even bother to look back.

She slapped the ground. Why hadn't he just said why he wanted to go alone, rather than being such a jerk about it, making it seem like he thought she was useless or he didn't want her around? And why did she care, anyway?

Alone now, she leaned against a tree, picked up a pine cone, and ripped off the scales one by one, flung them on the ground. Her face felt hot with an anger she couldn't explain. She needed Matt's help, but she couldn't let him think he could do whatever he wanted with her. When you trusted people like that, it would just come back to bite you. The only sound was the buzzing of insects. All day she'd wanted to be alone, but now that she was, it was far from peaceful. Closing her eyes, she felt tense and twitchy, as if she was going to jump out of her skin. Somehow, without her noticing, those insects had turned up the volume, and were so loud now that they sounded like the constant drone from a thousand power lines.

CHAPTER SIX

Emily woke with a jolt and her left leg jerked as if hit by an electric shock. Slumped against a tree trunk, it took a couple of seconds to realize where she was and that she'd fallen asleep. Dragging herself up, she shot a nervous glance around.

She was alone. Matt wasn't back.

Her throat felt dry, her tongue thick. Her head pounded. But she was still alive.

Sucking in a breath, she tried to decide how worried she should be. A couple of hours had passed, judging from the sun. It was just a pink smudge now, low in the sky, casting long and lonely shadows through the trees. There was an eerie stillness, as if everything had been shut down in preparation for night. Even the insects had abandoned her.

Shivering, she rubbed her arms, sorry now that she'd ditched the sweater a couple of hours earlier, when it had been so hot. She stretched her neck. Cold was the least of her worries. What if Matt was in trouble? What if he had been caught by those guys?

Running through the scenarios, her stomach tightened. He had gone off alone, because he had known it would be dangerous. And he had been caught. She slammed her fist on the ground, felt sharp bits of gravel bite into the skin. She should have gone with him. Why hadn't she? Had he been killed while she slept?

There was another possibility. He had decided not to come back. She nodded, said a silent prayer. That had to be it, because everything she knew about him indicated he wouldn't have easily been caught. A dead giveaway was the knapsack. He'd taken it. He wouldn't have done that if he were coming back.

Of course, there was the chance his reconnaissance mission had taken longer than expected. But that didn't make sense. The cove was close, just through the trees a bit. The smell of salt was in the air. Hadn't he said he'd be back in an hour? She racked her brain, couldn't remember.

Holding on to the tree trunk, she struggled to her feet, tried to think what to do. Water was a priority, which meant she had to find a cabin. A sound registered in her brain, like the scuffle of a shoe on rock. Her hands flew up to her face to cover her mouth as her heart leaped in her chest.

Stepping behind the tree, she reached down, grabbed the knife, and struggled with trembling hands to pry it open. What had he said? Don't worry about aiming, just use it. Taking a deep breath, she stepped away from the tree, ready to fight.

The man who walked toward her barely made any noise. He was tall, dark and, as he got closer, she could see his face bore traces of amusement.

Rambo.

Weak-kneed with relief, she stumbled back.

Gesturing to the knife, he said, "Can you put that down? You look like you want to use it on me."

She threw the knife away and fell against the tree. It took a minute to find her voice. "You scared the hell out of me."

He stepped toward her and reached out a hand, instantly contrite.

Jerking back, she held a palm up in warning for him not to come closer.

He handed her a bottle filled with water. "Drink as much as you want. I already had some and there's more in the knapsack."

Opening the bottle, she tipped it back and let the warm water slide down her parched throat. So that's why he'd taken the knapsack. "Where did you get it?"

"At a cabin. From an outdoor tap."

After another long drink, she said, "Is the cabin empty? Can we go there?" She wanted to sleep, eat if they could find anything, so she could get her strength back.

"I found something better."

"What?"

"A canoe. We should wait until dark before we cross to Egerton."

A rest sounded good, but getting to Egerton was better. But there was a false edge to his voice, barely perceptible, and something in the way he avoided her eyes made the hairs on her neck rise. She studied his face, knowing there was more. It certainly wasn't regret that he'd soon see the last of her.

She said, "What aren't you telling me?" He looked at her, surprised. "Tell me," she demanded.

"I nicked the canoe from a cottage about a mile up the shore. I can't be sure, but the owners may have seen me. They were partying on the deck. They could call the police."

"Do you think the police will come looking?"

He shook his head. "Probably not, but we can't be sure." He took a swig of water. "Maybe they'll just leave it until morning."

"We'll be long gone by that time. Did you see any boats? Any sign of those guys?"

"No. Let's keep our fingers crossed it will be all right."

Emily eyed him warily, didn't think he was lying. The beginnings of hope were like a little flutter in her belly. Maybe they would get to Egerton after all. Once separated, he would no longer be a target.

And he would be out of her life.

The realization didn't hit her like she'd expected. That flutter vanished, was quickly replaced by a dull ache that confused the hell out of her. That she was developing feelings for this guy, this macho man, had to be impossible. "Fingers crossed," she said, unsmiling.

Glancing up, she caught those heartbreaker eyes on her. Worse, that knowing look was back.

A flood of heat rushed to her face. How could he possibly

know what she was feeling? She didn't even know how to make sense of her rampaging emotions. Taking another gulp of water, she turned away. The light was fading fast, threatening to carry with it that sense of control so necessary to her survival.

* * *

At the cove, Matt scouted out a vantage point in the trees about twenty feet above the rocky shoreline as they waited for dark. They had ducked their heads in the water to wash off some dirt, and then Emily had found a couple of square feet of soft ground. She lay on her side with her head on one arm, the other arm pulled up close beside it. With her mouth slightly open, it looked like she was sleeping. He retrieved a thin nylon rain jacket out of the pack and covered her upper body, tucked it in around her neck. Somewhere along the line she must have ditched the sweater.

A sudden urge to lie down beside her and gather her in his arms swept through him like fire. He wanted to kiss her, hold her. Yes, even rip off that flimsy T-shirt.

His head buzzing, Matt forced his eyes away from her. How did this woman do this to him? That she was irritating as hell and seemed barely able to tolerate him didn't seem to matter.

He strode to the shoreline, sat down on a rock. He had a good view across the choppy water of the cove to Egerton. As it got darker, streetlights came on along a road that ran parallel to the touristy area of the downtown waterfront.

He dozed on and off for an hour, waited a while more until it was fully dark and woke Emily. They lifted the canoe off the ground above the shoreline and slipped it into the water. As he held it steady, she climbed in and crawled to the front. He threw the knapsack in the middle, climbed in, and pushed off the rocky shore with a paddle.

Emily gestured to a big cottage about a mile up the shore. Bright outside lights reflected green from the trees onto the black surface of the water. "Is that the cottage?"

He nodded. "I don't see anybody now. Maybe they took the party inside."

Emily glanced over her shoulder. "You really think we can do this in a couple of hours?"

"There's a good chance," he said in what he hoped was a confident tone. "The water looks pretty calm. It must be slack tide." The better question was whether they could cross without being seen. The light from the moon, not full but well over half, lit the glassy surface of the water like a giant floodlight. He shuddered, picturing a big boat speeding across the cove toward them.

The canoe jerked forward as they plunged their paddles into the water and then as they drew them back with long, swift strokes.

He said, "We have to be careful not to tip. The last thing we want to do is fall in. It's pretty cold, even at this time of year." Remembering her jump into the ocean that morning, he added, "Sorry, you know that all too well."

"Do I ever."

He paddled on toward the lights, as if he were in a race,

not letting himself slack off. Every six or seven strokes, he switched sides to keep the canoe straight, compensating for Emily. An hour later, by the time they were halfway across, his arms were sore. Not long after that, sharps needles of pain started shooting down from his shoulders to his wrists, even into his fingertips.

Needing a break, he pulled the paddle out of the water. "How are you doing?"

She stopped paddling, looked over her shoulder. Her face was pale in the moonlight. "I'm pretty sure I'm never getting in a canoe again in my life. The water feels thick as sludge."

He reached down, cupped some cold water in his hand, and splashed his face, tasting salt. "What will you do when we get to Egerton?"

"Find a place to sleep for the night." She gave a little smile. "You?"

"I'll figure out how I can go back and get my car."

Her mouth flew open. "I forgot about your car. I'm sorry."

"Don't worry about it. I'll get it somehow. Do you know anyone in Egerton?"

"No. But I'll be okay." She turned to the front again, put her paddle back in the water to stop further questioning.

He swallowed hard. It took great effort to not challenge that statement. She didn't have a cent on her and would rather die than ask him for money or help. It drove him crazy, although sometimes he saw glimpses of something else there, a vulnerability that showed the real person underneath. At least he thought he did. He had no luck reading this woman.

Emily let out a loud curse.

Tensing, he looked up. "What's wrong?"

"I think we have a welcoming party."

Squinting through the darkness, it took a few seconds to make out the police cruiser parked at the end of the wharf. Cursing, he slapped the water. *Would anything ever go their way?*

* * *

Matt pulled the paddle out of the water, tried to think. There was one cop in front of the cruiser, leaning against the hood. It was too far to see if there was another one in the car, not that it would make that much difference. This could go south very quickly.

Emily turned panicked eyes on him. "We have to go back."

"We can't. They could get a boat and chase us down."

"You can't turn me in." Her pleading eyes met his.

The cops were likely after the canoe, but he couldn't be sure. What if she was right and it was the police who were trying to kill her? Even if it was just a couple of rogue cops, it made any dealings with the police risky.

He said, "I won't turn you in." It felt all wrong, but he had no idea any more. He was navigating with a broken compass.

"Thanks." She let out a huge breath. "What are we going to do?"

"We have to get to shore, fast." But where? Ahead, bright lights lit up the water in front of the downtown. They wouldn't be able to slip ashore unseen.

Emily pointed about a mile down the shore to an area past the downtown core with fewer lights. "How about down there? What's that big building?"

"It's a hotel, sort of a resort. I've been there a few times. I seem to remember a sandy beach. But we'll have to be quick if we want to get there before the cops figure out where we're going."

Veering left, he swept his paddle through the water with a long stroke. A glance back caught the cop car driving off the wharf.

A few minutes later, her voice quaking, she said, "How did they find us?"

"Try not to worry. It might just be the canoe."

"They wouldn't go through this much trouble for a canoe." Her paddle chopped at the water with short, quick strokes.

"On a slow night they might." Or if the canoe belonged to somebody who could put up a stink, somebody like Egerton's mayor, who had a cottage in that area on the other side of the cove.

Soon, there were fewer lights. Arm muscles screaming, he concentrated his strokes on the left side to steer the canoe closer to shore. A few minutes later, the main building of the resort rose before them and they felt the bottom of the canoe hit sand. Jumping out, he waded through the water, helped Emily out, and pulled the canoe up on the beach. There was no time to hide it.

Crouching down, he peered through the tall grass near the water's edge across two hundred feet of manicured lawn to the hotel. The voices of people sitting around tables on a ground-floor patio drifted down to the cove. It was likely a bar or restaurant with some seating outside, but he couldn't recall. Other than that, there was nobody. Darkness shrouded the grounds, although bright lights lit the outside of the building.

He turned to Emily. "I'm going to get a car. Want to hitch a ride?" She mulled over the offer, but the doubt in her eyes quickly vanished. They crawled backed down to the beach, where they sprinted, heads down, about fifty feet up the sand to where the lawn ended and a wooded area that skirted the property began. It took a couple of minutes to run up the edge of the woods and sprint across a narrow strip of open lawn to the side of the hotel.

Panting, they crouched behind shrubs lining the side of the hotel foundation. There were no security guards that he could see.

She said, "How are we going to get a car?"

He avoided her look. "How do you think?"

"That's not funny."

"No choice. We have to get out of here quickly, before the cops come."

"If you steal a car, we'll get caught for sure." Frowning, she grabbed his arm. "Wait, how do you know how to steal a car?"

"I've got a perfectly good explanation. I'll tell you later. Right now, we have to get out of here."

She jumped up and down on the balls of her feet. "Shit."

He touched her shoulder. "Don't worry, we won't keep it. Just like the canoe."

Her eyes examined his face. "I don't want you to get into

trouble. They'll throw you in jail if they catch you."

His heart gave a kick. It wasn't much, a concern about getting him into trouble with the law more than anything. But it was something, something the softness in those green eyes couldn't hide.

Standing so close, he squeezed his eyes shut, fought an urge to touch her. When he opened them a second later, those big eyes, black with a halo of dark green, stared at him. The intensity was like oxygen on a fire smoldering deep inside him. His heart pounded in his chest. What if this was his last chance? If he didn't touch her now, she could slip away and he might never taste those lips.

Dipping his head, he cupped her chin in his hand and brushed his lips against hers. Her mouth was warm, salty. She sucked in a little breath and his tongue touched the tip of hers. Raw desire burning through him, he longed to bring her closer, to feel the length of her body against his. But he couldn't, not now anyway, and he forced himself to pull away.

Her expression was bewildered. "What was that all about?"

He didn't say anything, just watched those dark eyes, waited for the hammer to fall. But she didn't look angry, or scared, and she kept eye contact, didn't back away.

As if she hadn't minded it at all.

He turned around quickly, held that image before she remembered herself and put that wall back up between them.

"Car." Grabbing his arm, she dragged him behind a large rhododendron.

Through the leathery leaves of the shrub, he watched the car approach, knowing even before he saw the lights on the roof that it would be the cops. Emily, huddled against the white clapboard siding of the hotel, looked at him, terror in her eyes again.

He squeezed her hand. It was that kind of day. One step forward, two back.

CHAPTER SEVEN

Emily held her breath as the cruiser whipped past the side of the hotel and skidded to a stop at the front entrance. Seconds later, a car door slammed.

Matt waited two beats before he peeked around the corner. "He's gone inside. Let's go."

The parking lot held about fifty cars, angled into tight slots in three long bays. Light poles every dozen feet lit the lot up like a Christmas tree. She held back a curse. How the heck did he think he'd be able to steal one without getting caught?

With one eye on the hotel's front entrance, she crept after him up the far side of the parking lot. He stopped at the third bay, crouched down.

A car drove along the road toward the parking lot, the same way the cop car had come. It turned into the first bay, drove on to the second bay. She exchanged glances with Matt, and they crawled around to hide between two cars. After a few seconds, the purring of the engine stopped. Doors opened and the laughing voice of a woman cut through the night air. Sticking her head up, Emily watched a man put his arm around a woman who teetered in high heels, obviously drunk.

When the couple started walking to the hotel entrance, Matt got up, moved along to an old car in the middle of the bay. "Probably an employee car," he said when she had caught up. "I'd rather steal from the rich, but we wouldn't be able to hotwire a new one. You keep watch."

Putting the knapsack on the ground beside him, he took off a shoe. Emily peered over the trunk of the car beside them. Not seeing anything, she glanced at Matt, who had removed a shoelace. He made a loop and threaded it through the door.

She whispered, "Where did you learn this stuff? Or do I want to know?"

"I took a three-day course on escape and evasion. Never did get to use it overseas, but it's coming in handy right now."

He shot her a smile. Her stomach did that flip again, and warmth crept up her neck and into her face. He was gorgeous, so much so she couldn't take her eyes off him. "I'll have to sign up when this is over."

Easing the car door open, he fished a multi-tool out of his backpack, got in, and leaned across the seat. A few mumbled curses later, the car rumbled to life. The muffler sounded like somebody had dropped rocks in it. He snatched up his knapsack and motioned for her to get in the passenger side.

As she moved around the car, the cop came out the hotel's front entrance. Pulse pounding in her throat, she whispered a warning to Matt. Ducking down, they stared at each other, tried to listen for the cop but the car's muffler was too loud.

He said, "We have to go. We might attract more attention if we're idling in the parking lot and I don't want to shut it off. Duck down."

Heart beating furiously, she slid down in the seat. Matt picked up a ball cap from the backseat and put it on, then backed the car out and drove down the bay. The muffler made it sound like the car had tin cans attached, like a car with a sign bearing "Just Married" attached to it. The cop would stop them for sure.

Heart beating furiously, she said, "Is he watching?"

"Yes." He exhaled heavily. "I hope we don't have to make a run for it."

"Oh, God." He couldn't be serious. She felt the car turn left, and left again after ten long seconds. "Anything?"

Watching the rearview mirror, it was a half-minute before he answered. "You can get up now. He's not following."

She inched up, buckled her seat belt, waited for her heart to slow before speaking. "I just don't get it. Why are they going through so much trouble for a canoe?"

Avoiding her eyes, he scratched his head. "That was my fault."

"What do you mean?"

"It was a nice canoe, looked brand new. It's made of Kevlar."

"Kevlar? You picked a bullet-proof canoe? Did you think we were going to be shot at?"

"I had one once. They won't stop a bullet, but they're light and fast." A sheepish look was on his face. "But I think this one belonged to the mayor."

"What?"

"The mayor has a cottage on the other side of the cove."

Relief flooded through her. "You should have told me sooner. Here I was, sure the cops were after me."

"Will I redeem myself if I buy you a burger?"

"Can we risk it?"

"I think so. We'll get some coffee, too. We've got a long night ahead of us."

The road led them south, out of town, past a commercial area with gas stations, fast-food restaurants, and motels. He pulled up to a drive-through window at a fast-food restaurant and they ordered burgers, milkshakes, coffee, and water.

Back on the road, she watched a car come toward them, heading north. When it passed, she let out a breath, reached into the bag to open their meal.

The heady aroma of greasy food filled the car, but there was something to sort out first, something even more important than raging hunger. She turned to him. "Where are we going?"

He gave her a sly look, the corners of his mouth curving into a small smile. "Why, Emily, I think you're finally coming around to me. That's the first time you've used the word 'we,' at least in terms of us doing something together."

Shooting her a teasing smile, he looked seriously sexy, especially with that dark stubble on his chin. Feeling her face go red, she hoped it was too dark for him to see.

"Don't force your luck." She gave him a stern look. At least she hoped it was a stern look. It was hard controlling how she looked at him. Or how her body responded. "Let's put it this way, where are *you* going?"

Rubbing his chin, he considered this for a minute. "How

about this for a plan? We follow this road south for about an hour, and then we'll pick up the highway heading west into New Hampshire. If we drive all night, we should be in New Hampshire by morning. We'll stop at a motel, get cleaned up, maybe catch a couple hours of sleep. You should be able to get a bus to Riverton from there."

"And you'll head south to Boston?" For all her wanting to be clear of him, suddenly the thought of them parting brought a dull ache to her stomach. But she knew it had to happen. She couldn't let herself think of any other scenario.

He nodded. "I'll pick up a rental car in New Hampshire."

"Okay. Sounds like a plan," she said, that ache in her stomach deepening.

He smiled. "Can we eat now?"

Twenty minutes later, most of the food finished, she said, "I'll take a turn driving when you get tired."

"Okay, but you should sleep. You look beat."

Nodding, she put her head back against the headrest, closed her eyes. Her heart rate was in the normal range, but her mind raced with thoughts of her narrow escape. What would she do once she got to Riverton? Would it be safe to go to her apartment? She'd have to ask the landlord to let her in, since her keys were back at the cabin. But what if going there put other tenants at risk? No, she wouldn't go back there until this was all over.

Opening her eyes, she sat up straight. It was no use trying to sleep. The milkshake still cold in her hands, she sucked through the straw, finished it. The dim light made the mood in the car feel oddly intimate. Looking at Matt's large hands on the steering wheel, it wasn't hard to remember the feel of them on her face when he'd kissed her. Warm, gentle. Maybe some time those hands would touch her in a different way, one that was rougher, when his need was deeper.

What is with you?

To distract herself, she said, "Tell me about the woman you helped hide, the one whose husband was abusive."

"She was a friend of my sister's. I didn't know her that well." He shifted in his seat. "To hear her tell it, she married this guy and he changed overnight. First, she tried to stick with him—they'd had one of those huge weddings, it had cost her family a lot of money—but pretty soon she realized she couldn't."

He paused a few seconds. "She left him, but he kept coming around, begging her to take him back. When that didn't work, he said he'd kill her. She got a restraining order, but he didn't care. He spent a weekend in jail, got hold of a phone, and told her he was going to kill her when he got out. She believed him."

He ran a hand through his hair. "So we—my sister and I—decided to help her. We hid her out for a week while we set things up, got her a new identity. It wasn't easy, especially since she had a daughter. Anyway, so far, so good. My sister talks to her once in a while. She's moved on."

"Is she in contact with her family?"

"A bit and her ex remarried, so maybe she'd be okay. But she doesn't want to take chances."

"Why did you help her? It doesn't sound like an easy thing to do."

"It would have been easier to just break his neck, or at least put a good scare into him, but that wouldn't have been smart. In a way, it benefited me, too."

"What do you mean? Did you have something going on with this woman?"

He scoffed. "No, it's because of her that I'm doing what I'm doing. She had some money, but nowhere near enough to buy a house, and I realized there was a niche market, especially in cities. My company specializes in small, energy efficient designs for low-income people and retirees, or just people who don't want to live in a big house. There's more money to be made building bigger houses, but I get a lot more satisfaction out of this."

They picked up the highway heading inland, a long gray ribbon winding west across the state through farmland and forest. The traffic was sparse, mostly trucks. No cop cars.

She fell asleep, waking just before four in the morning when Matt stopped for gas at a twenty-four-hour station. While she went to the washroom, he filled the gas tank and bought coffee for her.

Back in the car, she took the wheel.

"We should be in New Hampshire in a couple of hours," he said. "Pull into the first old motel you see. We'll stop, get cleaned up, get some new clothes, and rest up before we get back on the road."

She thought about asking him why it had to be old, but let it go.

A minute later, he was asleep, as if he'd just flicked a switch. She wished she could sleep like that. Just before sunrise she crossed into New Hampshire, although it took another twenty minutes before she spotted an old motel. At least the sign was old, the words Carport Motel painted in faded black letters on a weathered sign.

As she pulled off the road, he woke up, rubbed his face. "Where are we?"

"Half an hour over the border. I found an old motel. And there's a mall and a car rental place over there." She pointed across the highway.

The motel was a single-level, U-shaped building with a parking lot in the middle. At the front of one end was a diner with a dozen cars out front. There was no sign of a carport. She parked the car out of sight behind a truck and waited while Matt got a room. When he came back, they left the car where it was and walked to a room in the middle of the U at the back. The small room had thin green carpet, two double beds, and two tub chairs on either side of a small table next to the window. A door in the middle of one wall led to an adjoining room. She checked to ensure it was locked.

Matt passed her an extra-large men's T-shirt with "New Hampshire" printed on it. "They were selling them in the lobby. It was the only size they had. I got one for you, one for me."

"It's great. I'm going to take a shower." In the shower, she scrubbed herself with a little bar of soap. There was no shampoo, so she used soap on her hair. The T-shirt was long enough to cover her butt, which was all she cared about.

When she came out, Matt smiled. "You could fit five of you in there."

She smiled. "It's not exactly what a bride would wear on her wedding night."

She meant it to be a light remark, but he just stared at her, naked need in his eyes. "You could be wearing the proverbial potato sack. You know that, don't you?"

Feeling her cheeks warm, she looked away. Men just didn't look at her like that. Not that she gave them the chance. Usually a hard stare was enough to make them turn away. So why wasn't she using that stare now?

He went into the bathroom, turned on the shower, the water sounding like rain sluicing over that hard body. She imagined him dipping his head under the showerhead to wash his hair. Those large hands soaping his muscular chest and arms.

Climbing under the covers, she felt the heat of him on her body like a fever. He didn't even have to say anything. That look was enough.

She squeezed her eyes shut. A couple of more hours, that's all she had to get through. After that, she'd be on a bus, moving on.

* * *

Someone was on the walkway in front of their room. Rolling out of bed, Matt crept to the window, flicked back a corner of the curtain. An elderly couple entered the room next to them.

Letting out a breath, he checked his watch. It was just before noon, which meant he had slept for more than four hours. He snuck a glance at Emily. She was sleeping on her side, curled up with her hands tucked under her head on the pillow. Soft lips lightly touching, she looked totally relaxed. An urge to walk over and stroke that soft skin overwhelmed him.

Who was he fooling? Physical contact with her was a very a dangerous idea. He was barely hanging on to control as it was. His throat feeling tight, he forced himself to turn away.

Sitting down on the bed, he slipped the clean tourist T-shirt over his head and pulled on his dirty khaki shorts. They needed some clothes, food, and another car. They'd have to find out where he could put her on a bus. God, he didn't want to do that. But he had to. Walking over, he nudged her awake.

For a moment it seemed she didn't know where she was. She laid perfectly still, eyes darting around the room before they stopped on him on the bed opposite her. Sitting up against the headboard, she pulled the cover over her, rubbed her eyes. "What time is it?"

"Almost noon." He stood up. "I'm going to go to the mall across the street to pick up a car, get some clothes and stuff. Then we can get something to eat at the diner."

"Maybe somebody there will know where I can pick up a bus to Riverton," she said.

"We'll ask. Do you want to come shopping?"

She shook her head. "I'd rather not get back into dirty clothes, if you don't mind."

Leaving the stolen car in the motel lot, he crossed the four-lane highway at a set of traffic lights, walked down to the car rental agency, and signed out a small blue hatchback. At the department store, he grabbed a cart and spent ten minutes tossing in toiletries and clothes, and another five minutes in the women's underwear section before settling on a stretchy sports bra. In the checkout line, he remembered her blister and went back and picked up a pair of sandals, guessing her size.

Back at the motel, he parked in front of one of the rooms on the other side of the U, walked over to the stolen car, and took five minutes to wipe it for prints, knowing his would be on file from his days in the military. That finished, he knocked on the door and waited for Emily to release the chain to let him in.

Thanking him, Emily grabbed a T-shirt, shorts, and underwear and went into the bathroom to change. When she emerged five minutes later, the clothes looked at least a size too big but she didn't seem to care. He used the bathroom to shave and change his clothes.

At the diner, which was nearly full with a lunchtime crowd, they found a booth near the back. The waitress, a middle-aged woman who moved with the efficiency of someone who'd spent years on the job, dropped off menus and came back a few minutes later with coffee and took their orders.

When she'd gone, he said with a teasing smile, "I didn't know chefs ate burgers and fries. Last night you didn't have much of a choice, but you do now."

She took a sip of coffee. "Just because I work as a chef, doesn't mean I'm a food snob. Besides, it will be fast and hot and I'm way too hungry for a salad."

The same waitress brought soup to a middle-aged couple in a booth across from them. The woman leaned over, said something to the man, and he took off his ball cap and set it down on the seat. Matt turned to Emily. Scrubbed clean, she looked young and fresh. He loved the way she absentmindedly touched the scar on her forehead. And so beautiful it took his breath away. He swallowed, tried to put the thought she would soon be out of his life out of his mind. "Tell me more about your family. You haven't mentioned your father."

"My father died when I was eight. A heart attack. My mother is my family."

"That must have been tough."

"My father had a lot of stress, from his job. He owned two hotels and he worked all the time. He was wealthy but he never really got to enjoy it. And he spent so much time working, I never really felt close to him."

The waitress came with their food. He took a bite of his club sandwich. "Your mom runs the hotels?"

"She sold one, kept the other. She's a good businesswoman, works very hard. Runs a tight ship." She smiled wistfully. "She's very different from me, very social, extroverted. She's like you in a way, has to have everything planned out."

He grimaced. "You don't make that sound like a good thing."

She speared a French fry with her fork. "I didn't mean it to be. She just does what she has to do to get the job done. It was very hard for her after my father died, being a single parent and running a big hotel. I looked after myself a lot, moved away when I was eighteen, and went to college."

"So you're very independent."

"I learned early on the value of looking after myself. Amber always said I brought myself up. In some ways I was closer to Amber than to my own mother."

"But you came back to Riverton?"

"A year ago, my mother asked me to work as a chef at the

hotel. I had done a year of law school and needed to make some money to be able to go back. It didn't really think I would stay working for my mother. But she can be very persuasive."

He finished his club sandwich and pushed the plate away. "Will you go back to law school?"

"I think so, as soon as I extricate myself from my mother." She made concentric circles with the bottom of a wet water glass on the table. "She's got a boyfriend. I think I told you about him. They've been together a few years, so that might make it a bit easier."

The waitress picked up their empty plates and said she'd be back with the bill. He turned to Emily. "What's the boyfriend like?"

"They were friends for years, but now it seems to be developing into something more serious. I don't know him that well. He's a judge, very reserved. She likes him, that's what matters."

After a while, Matt said, "Tell me more about your cousin. What was she like?"

"She was wonderful, smart, and principled. She was an addiction counselor for teenagers and she was really good at it. She really believed in standing up for the little guy."

"But she got addicted to drugs herself?"

"Happens more than you think. But she got off them. It took time, but she was clean."

"How old was she?"

"She was three years older than me, twenty-seven when she died." She brushed a stray strand of hair back from her forehead. "But we always got along really well. Our mothers are sisters. And they're the same, hard to please. She got along better with me than she did with her sister. We could really understand each other."

"Tell me about her sister."

"Celia's about as unlike Amber as you can imagine. She's very confident, focused, interested in making money. Amber liked reading and hiking. Celia's a partier. She sells real estate, and she's very good at it, keeps winning awards for selling so many of them."

"Do you get along with this Celia?"

"I'm kind of on her shit list right now. She told me I was sticking my nose where it didn't belong and upsetting her mother."

"What did you say to that?"

"I didn't have a chance to say anything. We were talking in my apartment. Celia got up and left. She slammed the door on her way out."

The waitress dropped off the bill. After leaving a tip, they made their way to the cash register near the front door. A television on the wall behind the counter was tuned to a news station. The volume was off, but the announcer's words streamed across the bottom of the screen. A picture of a young woman flashed on the screen. Something about her eyes hinted at a resemblance to Emily.

The bill paid, he turned to Emily, who watched the television with a desperate look in her eyes. His heart squeezed.

The announcer said the death of Riverton resident Amber Williams was now being treated as a homicide. She said a man was being interviewed by police and showed a video clip of a guy being escorted into the police station. It cut to a clip of the police chief.

"That's Jason, Amber's boyfriend," she said, her voice barely above a whisper, as the announcer switched to the next item.

They walked out into the parking lot. Emily had her head down, seemed to be trying to digest the information. She didn't say anything, but he could almost see the wheels in her head turn.

When she looked up, her eyes were wet. "How could he?"

"I don't know, but they must have some evidence against him."

"I have to find out what it is. I have to talk to the police chief. That was him on TV."

He grimaced. "What if it's a trap?" What if she was right about not being able to trust the cops?

"What do you mean? What kind of a trap? They wouldn't announce they had a suspect if they didn't have something."

His stomach knotted. "They didn't say he was a suspect. Just that they were interviewing a man. That could mean anything."

"I still have to find out." She stopped at the passenger side of their rental car, her hands in fists at her side. "Did you ask where the bus station is?"

He walked away from the car. An idea that had been slowly building came into sharp focus. He couldn't let her face this alone. Who was he kidding? He'd known as soon as he woke in the hotel room and watched her sleeping he couldn't bear never seeing her again. It was no use trying to talk himself out of what he knew he was going to do.

Walking back, he stood in front of her, dipped his head to meet her eyes. "I'll go with you."

She shook her head. "Why would you do that?"

"You know the saying, if you save someone's life, you're responsible for them forever? That's what it's like. I'm invested in you."

Scowling, she rolled her eyes. "That's the biggest line of crap I've ever heard. You barely even know me."

"You might not like the real answer."

"What real answer?" She gave him a blank look. "What are you talking about?"

There was no choice but to come out and say it. "I'm beginning to like you a lot. I don't want to see anything bad happen to you."

She backed up into the car. "I can't let you do this. You don't even know me. You don't know how messed up I am. How messed up my life is."

"More messed up than this?" He gave a little smile.

Her shoulders slumped. "Actually, yeah, and it's going to get even get messier."

"Just let me take you to Riverton, no strings attached. We'll see after that." He gestured to the direction of their motel room, cutting off further argument. "Let's get our stuff."

They walked back to the room, stuffed their belongings into plastic bags. Emily waited in the car while he went off to pay for the room.

When he returned, she gave him a long look. "You don't have to do this."

"I know."

She met his gaze for a moment, her eyes reflecting a mixture of hope and despair. "Okay, I agree, but you have to understand that you're not responsible for my safety. And you can back out at any time."

Nodding, he started the car, smiled to himself. Maybe he had a chance after all.

And it didn't matter what kind of conditions she put on it. He did feel responsible. She was one gutsy woman, and she would see this through to the end. So would he.

Even if it meant walking into a setup, because some instinct told him it was. And he always paid attention to his instinct.

CHAPTER EIGHT

Clutching her arms to her chest, Emily stared through the side window of the rental car. It had started raining by the time they got back on the road, and tiny beads of water distorted the mountains and forests outside the window like an impressionist painting.

Matt glanced over. "What are you thinking about?"

She couldn't tell him. The fact that he was putting his life at risk for her burned a hole in her stomach. It made her realize her feelings were a lot more complicated than she'd thought. She wanted him out of her life, safe. But that was her mind talking. Her body was telling her something different. When he was around, every nerve in her body came alive.

Realizing he was waiting for an answer, she pinched her lips together, forced her mind back to Jason's arrest. "It doesn't make sense. I wonder what sort of evidence the police have, because I find it hard to get my head around the idea that Jason killed Amber. I mean, what would his motive be? They seemed to be really in love."

"We'll try to find that out today. They must have something to go on."

"If it's true—and that's a big if—in some ways it would be a relief." She rubbed the back of her neck. The windshield wipers thumped back and forth in a soft rhythmic dance. "On the other hand, if he didn't do it, we'd be back to square one."

He reached over, squeezed her hand. "Can you call your mom? See what she knows?"

She shook her head. "She won't talk to me about it." He shot her a puzzled look, but she didn't want to explain, at least not now.

They reached Riverton just before four in the afternoon and drove straight to the police station, a two-story redbrick building near the downtown area. At the counter, she asked to see the chief about Amber's case and waited while the secretary made a telephone call. When she got off the phone, the woman said the chief was busy but a detective would see them if they were willing to wait. They sat down in a small waiting room.

"Can I get you a coffee?"

She tapped her fingers on the arm of the chair. "No, thanks, I'm already too jittery."

He asked a few questions about Jason Hatt, but there wasn't much she could tell him. Leaning back in his chair, he closed his eyes, stretched his legs out in front of him. She flipped through half a dozen magazines without interest, tried to ignore her churning stomach.

Forty minutes later, a tall, slim man walked up to them. After introductions, Detective Sam Fisher led them down a long, narrow hallway to a small room at the back of the building. There were three chairs and a desk in the room, and it looked like it was used for interviewing suspects, with a two-way mirror, nothing on the walls, uncomfortable chairs. Everything about it seemed designed to put people on edge. Fisher took the chair behind the desk and they sat across from him.

Fisher put a manila file folder, unopened, on the desk in front of him. "You asked for an update on the Amber Williams case investigation." He looked at the folder, adjusted it with his fingertips until it was lined up straight. Satisfied, he looked up. "A week ago, I was asked to review the evidence."

No explanation was offered for why he was asked to review the case, and she made a mental note to ask that question later.

Fisher continued. "The first officers at the scene thought it was a suicide. They saw Ms. Williams' body in her bathtub, empty pill bottles nearby on the counter. No sign of a struggle. In ninety-nine percent of these cases, it is suicide."

Matt tilted his head to the side. "Are you saying that they made assumptions they shouldn't have?"

After a glance at Matt, Fisher turned back to Emily, ignoring the question. She shot Matt a glance, wondered just how much information they'd be able to squeeze out of the detective.

Fisher said, "I should also note that our initial contact with the victim's family pointed to suicide or accidental overdose. Her sister, Celia Williams, said she saw her taking prescription medication about a week before her sister died."

Gripping the bottom of the armless chair, she said, "That's not true." Celia had to be lying. Emily had seen Amber herself a couple of days before she died and knew Amber was clean.

His expression didn't change. "I'm just telling you the facts as they were given. The victim's mother, and your mother, told us when they were interviewed that they believed it was suicide."

Swallowing, she didn't say anything, wished he would skip the part about what the family thought. That they had tried to discourage her from pushing for a murder investigation she already knew, but not that they'd lobbied to have it shut down. Not that that should have had much effect on the police investigation, although it seemed that it might have.

Matt said, "What happened to change that initial ruling of suicide or accidental death?"

"There was no note, which in itself isn't unusual, but when we interviewed all the witnesses a second time, problems surfaced with Jason Hatt's alibi. He claimed he was with another woman, but she's not what you call the most reliable witness."

Her mouth fell open. "Another woman? Who is she?"

"I can't say." His poker face gave nothing away.

That churning in her stomach increased. "Was he having an affair?"

"I can't say."

Matt said, "But why would he kill Amber? Did she find out about this other woman?"

Fisher cleared his throat. "We're still pinning down a motive."

Emily sat forward, her mind reeling. "What about the attack on me? I know that wasn't Jason."

"Can you give us proof that it wasn't? As I recall, you were unable to give a good description—"

"I was attacked, and it was night." Aware she'd raised her voice, she made an effort to lower it. "But I still know it wasn't Jason. The man who hit me was shorter."

"He may have involved somebody else."

Matt said, "Do you have any other evidence on Jason Hatt?"

"We're working on it."

Matt scrubbed a hand over his face. "What about the autopsy?"

"The pathologist found no evidence of homicide. There were no marks on the body or any sign of violence. The lab reports showed a combination of three drugs, at levels high enough to kill her. But, like I said, there was no evidence to suggest that anyone else was involved."

She stared at the detective, scrambling to understand. "It sounds like you don't have a lot to go on."

"These things take time. We're awaiting results of some tests."

The cell phone the detective was wearing on his belt buzzed. Answering it, he listened a moment before he said, "Be right out." He finished the call and got to his feet. "I have another meeting."

Following the detective to the door, she looked at Matt. His narrowed eyes indicated the same confusion that had her heart racing. Something about it didn't smell right. Correct that. Everything about it didn't smell right. Expecting answers, instead she had more questions. Was Jason being set up? Or did he really do it? Why would he lie about his alibi?

They walked in silence to the front waiting area. A woman stood at the counter. Emily tensed. Celia, Amber's sister, was talking to Frank Cameron, the police chief. She looked every inch the professional in a crisp white shirt, gray pencil skirt, her long, curly brown hair pulled back in a ponytail. Her lipstick was deep red, almost maroon. Black high heels made her almost as tall as the chief.

Celia turned to look at them, a flicker of unease in her eyes. After saying something to the chief, she walked over, her gaze lingering on Matt for a second too long before it came to Emily.

Celia said, "I see you're back in town. What are you doing?"

She spoke quickly, and her voice had a crisp edge that she likely used for clients. There was something else there, too, something darker. A chill gripped her heart. The casual indifference she had long received from Celia had morphed into open dislike, even hatred.

Taking a breath, she introduced Matt before answering the question. "Performing my civic duties. You?"

"Not bad, all things considered. Mother's in France. She had to get away from all this. I thought about joining her, but I'm too busy at this time of year."

Nodding, Emily started to walk away, but Celia said, "We all miss Amber, not just you. But we have to face up to the fact that she did this to herself."

The chill in her heart turned to ice. She couldn't think what to say, realized nothing would change Celia's mind.

What had Amber done to deserve such cruelty?

Celia lifted her red lips into a small smile. "You asked what I'm doing here. I'm moving on with my life. Frank is buying one of my listings. He just got a divorce and needs a house."

Lucky for you.

Celia walked back to the chief, a wiry man in his fifties who stood next to the counter, watching. Catching Emily's eye, he dipped his head in a small nod.

She'd met with Cameron once to discuss Amber's case and hadn't made her mind up about him. Watching him walk off down the hall with Celia, one thing became plainly obvious. That chill wrapped itself tighter around her heart.

She couldn't trust either one of them.

* * *

Outside, Matt glanced at Emily as they walked to the car. Her eyes glistened with tears and dark thoughts moved like shadows across her face.

She kicked the tire of the car. "That got us a whole lot of nowhere."

"I'd have to agree with you there." That he wasn't surprised, and that it smelled liked a cover-up, he kept to himself.

Standing beside the rental car, he glanced up at the windows of the police station. Someone watched them from the second floor.

"Let's get out of here." He unlocked the car doors. "There's a park down the street. We can talk there."

A few minutes later, when they stepped onto a gravel path

at the entrance to the park, she said, "The detective sounds like he doesn't have anything beyond Jason Hatt's questionable alibi. I'd like to know who gave it, and what the problem is."

"We'll go talk to him, see if he'll tell us."

They followed the winding path for a minute without speaking. It ran alongside a large, formal flower bed, blooms of purple and yellow arranged in neat vertical lines. The late-afternoon sun sparkled through the leaves of the gigantic trees towering above them.

She said, "I keep thinking things would have been different if the first cops hadn't screwed up."

"I agree with you there. From what the detective said, it sounds like they had tunnel vision. They assumed it was suicide and didn't consider other possibilities."

"But that's what I don't understand. Fisher pretty well implied that they screwed up, but at the same time he didn't seem to have any evidence that it wasn't suicide or an accident."

"Maybe there's something he's not telling us. Something about the autopsy or about the results they're still waiting for."

At a park bench, she sat down, looked across when he joined her. "What did you think of Celia?"

"It's hard to get a full picture from just meeting her once, but she didn't show very much regard for her sister." He held back what he really thought, that Celia seemed like a real piece of work. It was hard to imagine she was related to Emily. Remembering that lipstick, he shuddered. It reminded him of the color of dried blood.

"I can't believe she told them Amber was using again. I know she wasn't."

"Why would she lie?"

"I don't know." Emily rubbed her head in her hands.

Walking again, he said, "Or could it be something else?"

She looked at him, puzzled. "What do you mean? That Celia killed her? I don't know if I can believe that."

"No, but maybe she knew who did it or why, and had a reason to cover it up."

"It might explain her behavior, but it's still hard to believe. And what about Amber's mom and my mother? Why would they cover it up?"

"Maybe they really believed Amber killed herself. Or they didn't want an investigation. It wouldn't bring Amber back."

"That's not a good reason to bury the truth." After a silence, she said, "I just don't think Jason did it."

"You might be right, but he still could know something he's not telling." He clenched his jaw. "Right now, it looks like we're no closer to the truth."

Seeing his frustration, she stopped and faced him. "Matt, you don't have to stay."

"You don't want me to?" His breath caught in his chest.

"I'm not saying that. But I really have no idea what's going to happen next."

Letting out a big breath, he said, "I'm staying. We're in this together."

"Thank you. I really don't know what to do. I hoped this would all be over, but right now it looks worse. We can't trust anybody."

Up ahead, five or six teenagers in dark clothing lounged on the grass beside the path. Two boys watched Emily as they approached. They looked away when Matt stared them down.

Oblivious to the attention, Emily said, "I can't wait until this is all over and I can get out of this town. Everybody's just a bit too close for comfort."

Back at the car, he glanced at her as he put the key in the ignition. "What now?"

"I have to go see my mother. What? Why are you looking at me like that?"

"Just a feeling you're not looking forward to it."

"You don't know my mother."

He had picked up a prepaid cell phone earlier and handed it to Emily, getting out of the car while she made the call. A man jogged out of the park and up the sidewalk. A golden retriever ran beside him, a lime green rubber toy, maybe an alligator, between its teeth.

A minute later, Emily finished the call and he got back in the car.

She said, "I called her cell. She'll be home in an hour." She described where her mother lived, about twenty minutes away, and they decided to stop at a downtown café to grab a bite to eat.

Later, after they'd had soup and a salad and walked back to the car, she said, "Maybe they all know something I don't. Something about Amber they didn't want to tell me. Maybe she was having problems with Jason. Maybe I got it all wrong."

"I don't think so. Don't forget that you were attacked. And tracked down to that cabin. I keep thinking back to that. You were very careful, but somehow they tracked you down. If we could find out how, it may be the clue we need."

"But not even my mother knew. I didn't want to put her in any danger. I thought it would be best if she didn't." She laughed derisively. "Besides, she can't keep a secret. She's the world's greatest gossip. I wouldn't trust her with information like that."

"What did you tell her when you left?"

"I just said I had to take a vacation. At first she was angry, threatened to fire me, but she came around to the idea."

"But she knew your life was in danger? She knew about the attack?"

"She said I was overreacting, that it was random. There had been an attack on a woman a week or two before not far from where I was attacked."

He shook his head slowly side to side. How could her mother react like that?

They pulled onto the street where Emily's mother lived. It had big old houses with verandahs and two- or three-car garages, not at all like his old neighborhood. They stopped in front of her mother's place, a three-story Victorian.

"Did you grow up here?" It had a spindle-work porch and decorative trim, but was robbed of any folksy charm by somber gray-green wood siding.

She nodded. "It's ridiculously big. She tried to sell it a few years ago, but I guess she was asking too much. It's too big for most families. And it has a heritage designation, so it's hard to get approval to do any renovations."

He said, changing the subject, "When you were being chased out of your cabin, and I was on the mainland, taking pictures, I actually took some of you and those guys."

She perked up. "Do you think there's something on there?"

"I don't know. I looked at the pictures this morning while you were sleeping, couldn't see anything. It was pretty dark and far away, but we could find somebody who could take a look at them, see if they can enhance them."

The corners of her lips lifted into a small smile. "It's worth a try."

"Why don't you visit with your mother and I'll make some calls about the pictures. I'll find us a motel, too. It's too risky to go to your apartment. I'll be back in an hour or so, okay?"

"I need to get to a bank. I can't keep letting you pay for everything."

"We can get to one tomorrow, but don't worry about the money. It's not an issue."

Nodding, she got out of the car, walked slowly to the front door. He waited until she was inside before driving off, realizing with a pang of fear that an hour was too long to be away. She was in her mother's house, but that didn't offer much reassurance.

CHAPTER NINE

W hat did you do to your hair?"

Emily's mother stood in the doorway, her expression suggesting a kind of mortified shock that was all too familiar. The best response, Emily had learned as a teenager, was no response. She used this tactic now, and after a long moment her mother stepped aside to let Emily in.

"And your clothes?" her mother said when she had shut the door, not ready to give up yet. "They look like they came from a thrift shop."

"You don't like the look?" Emily slipped off her sandals and leaned up to kiss the pale cheek her mother presented. They were the same height but her mother had the advantage of four-inch heels.

"It's ghastly." A chilly glance slid up and down her daughter's body. She let out a frustrated sigh. "You look like you've lost weight."

Emily gave a small smile, realizing the preoccupation with

her weight meant the big bandage on her blistered foot had escaped notice.

They walked to the living room, her mother's heels clicking down the black-and-white-tiled hallway. She gestured to armless leather chairs by the front windows. Emily lifted her right foot to tuck it under the other leg on the chair but stopped herself, planted both feet on the floor. A bad habit, and one her mother wouldn't overlook.

"You look well," Emily said, meaning it. Nearing fifty, her mother was a beautiful woman with delicate features, and trim and fit. Today, her dyed blond hair was pulled back in a sleek ponytail and her blouse, a rich royal blue, brought out the blue in her eyes and the sapphire stones in her tennis bracelet.

"Why, thank you, my dear." Her mother smiled cheerfully. "I hope you've come to tell me that you're coming back to work soon."

Biting the inside of her cheek, not ready for that fight today, Emily decided to stall. "I'm not sure."

"It will be good for you. You know I only want what's best for you." She picked a piece of lint off her pants. "I hope you still aren't thinking about going back to law school. Aunt Jean is finalizing Amber's insurance case from the accident. It's very upsetting. It looks like half of it will go to the lawyer."

"I wouldn't go into law to make money."

"That's what they all say."

Emily smiled tightly, wondering why she had bothered.

"I was talking earlier with Celia. She's been doing so well lately. She was named one of the firm's top ten agents last month. Did you hear that? It was for the whole state."

"No, I didn't," she said, recognizing the tactic. Instead of saying outright what a disappointment Emily was, her mother would underline her shortcomings by comparing her to someone truly worthy, usually Celia. The conclusion left for Emily to draw was hard to miss.

"Celia said she ran into you at the police station. What were you doing there?" Waiting for a reply, she pursed her lips.

Emily, trained to watch for signs, answered cautiously. "Getting an update on the investigation."

"And? Are you satisfied finally?" She twisted the bracelet on her wrist.

Taking a breath, she shook her head. "No."

"Really, Emily, this is getting old."

Sucking in a slow, deep breath, she willed herself not to get angry and met her mother's glassy stare. "Why did you try to stop the investigation in Amber's death?"

"I didn't try to stop any investigation. I just gave my opinion when I spoke to Frank. Surely, I'm entitled to that?" Her tone was sharp.

She ignored the question, storing away for future reference the fact that her mother was on a first-name basis with the police chief. "Do you think Jason killed her?"

"The fact of the matter is Amber was on drugs. She overdosed. Whether on purpose or by accident, we don't know." She paused, calming a bit. "Even if she was helped, what good would it do to find out why? It would just bring more pain. Why do you have to be so bloody stubborn about this?"

Emily felt a chill run through her. Why was it so hard to understand it wasn't over until Amber had justice? Never mind that someone had attacked her, that men had chased her, tried to kill her.

Her mother said, "Your aunt, my sister—the only sister I have—wants it to be over. But now it's being raised again and you know she's not a strong woman. If you went about it differently, I could see, but you always seem to make a mess of things. Celia tells me that you've even dragged some man into this."

"I didn't drag him into it." She took another deep breath. The last thing she wanted was to discuss Matt.

"Well, how did you meet him?"

"Actually, he saved my life."

Face flooding with anger, her mother glared at her. "Not this again."

The look her mother gave her—eyes narrowed, lips pressed into a white line—together with the high-pitched tone in her voice stopped her cold. A rush of memories from her childhood flooded her. The details were a blur, but not that terrible suffocating feeling that resulted from being on the receiving end of her mother's anger. She felt it now in the crushing pressure on her chest, as if a ton of rocks had fallen on her.

Emily turned away, squeezed her eyes shut. She wasn't going to cry. No way.

The telephone rang in the kitchen. Scowling, her mother sprang up, went off to answer it.

Emily took a deep breath and looked around. She hated this room. Growing up, she'd only been allowed in to be reprimanded. The furnishings had changed over the years. Now it was starkly modern, everything white, including the pickled white stain on the floors.

Ten minutes later, her mother came back. "That was Harold. He's stopping by." She walked to the window, looked out onto the street. "Perhaps you could stay to say hello."

"All right." It was safer with people around. Usually, but not always, the harshest rebukes were saved for when her mother had her alone. "How is he?"

"He's fine, busy." Hesitating, she pinched the skin on her neck. "I may as well tell you, we are planning to be married. But please keep that under your hat for the time being."

"I'm happy for you, Mother."

Sitting down, her mother crossed her legs. A bitter smile played across her lips. "Yes, well, we can't set a date until this business with Amber is finished."

An awful, sinking feeling puddled in Emily's stomach. She was to blame for messing her mother's life up once again. Her mother stared at her, waiting for her to say something. Emily stood up. "I'm going upstairs for a minute. There are some clothes in the closet I'd like to take." She took a few steps before turning around. "By the way, the friend Celia mentioned is coming by to pick me up."

"Boyfriend?"

"He's just a friend." In the hallway, there was a large painting on the wall, a sort of abstract expressionist work with squiggly black lines, layers and layers of them, on a stark white canvas.

Her mother called out from across the room, "I just bought it at an auction. It cost a pretty penny. I'm not sure I like it, but it's an investment."

Walking upstairs, she wondered if her mother saw her as an investment. As a daughter, she was a flop, but there was still some value in her as a chef.

Going away to college had been one of the best things she'd ever done; coming back to work for her mother had been a big mistake.

* * *

Mona Blackstock answered the door when Matt returned an hour after he'd dropped Emily off. She introduced herself with a stiff smile, led him into the living room, where Emily stood by the window, her arms crossed tightly in front of her. He wanted to go to her, but Mona gestured to a pair of sofas set up across from each other in front of a tiled fireplace.

"What exactly is it that you do?" she asked after she had sat down across from him, her back to her daughter. "Emily didn't say."

He shot a glance at Emily, but she'd turned to look out the window. Something had happened before he had arrived. Tension hung in the air. "I work with a company in Boston, building houses."

"Really, how interesting."

Her tone suggested about as much interest as a six-year-old might have in a plate of mashed turnips. "Emily tells me you're in the hotel business."

"I own the Carleton, near the downtown. Have you been?"

"Haven't had the chance yet." He wondered if the hotel had a similar decor to this room. Everything white, it had all the warmth of a dentist's waiting room and a peculiar smell, too, like furniture polish mixed with disinfectant.

The room suited its owner. It wasn't hard to see where Emily had gotten her looks, but Mona gave off a chilly, hard-edged composure that made him sit upright in his seat.

She was talking about the hotel. "It's a lovely old building. We are very proud of it, aren't we, Emily?" She didn't wait for a response. "It has just six floors but one hundred and seventy-seven rooms. It's certainly a lot of work."

The doorbell rang. Without turning around, Mona said, "That will be Harold. Emily, be a dear and get it."

Emily shot him a smile as she walked across the room to the hallway. The conversation died. Behind Mona, a huge frame stood against the wall. There was nothing in it, and it looked antique, although he suspected it wasn't really, but had been beaten with chains and painted a dozen times to make it look old. It would have looked better if it had something in it, preferably something very colorful. But that was just his opinion. What did he know?

Emily returned with a tall, barrel-chested man in his early sixties. Salt-and-pepper hair and a neatly trimmed mustache gave him a distinguished air. Harold MacDonald exchanged introductions with Matt, who stood to greet him, leaned down to kiss Mona on the cheek, and sat beside her. Emily joined Matt on the sofa across from Mona and the judge.

The judge asked him about home construction. His questions were knowledgeable, and he explained he had recently moved into a custom new build on a five-acre plot of land on a small mountain a few miles north of town. From the description, it sounded very big and very expensive.

Mona, waiting for a break in the conversation, turned to Matt. "Emily and I just had a discussion, and I think we agreed on the importance of not overreacting."

Emily stiffened beside him but said nothing, so he said, "I don't know what you've discussed, but I haven't seen Emily overreacting to anything. I'm concerned for her safety, in fact." He reached over, squeezed Emily's hand. Her delicate lips lifted in a small smile and when she returned the squeeze his heart did strange things in his chest.

Mona said, "Really? You don't know Emily like I do. In fact, how long have you known her?"

"A little while." She threw out the word "really" a lot, in a way that implied she severely doubted the veracity of what he said. He said, before she could say more, "Do you know why Jason Hatt is a suspect?"

Shaking her head, she looked in the judge's direction. "Harold, do you?" Looking back at Matt, she added, "Harold is a judge. He sometimes knows about such things."

MacDonald shrugged. "Sorry, no, I haven't kept up on that case." He looked at Emily. "But if you believe there are valid reasons to be concerned for your own safety, you shouldn't ignore them. I once got a threatening letter from somebody I sent to prison. It wasn't pleasant."

Mona said, "Harold's new home has a very expensive security system. It even has a safe room. It'll be harder to break into than Fort Knox."

"I don't know about that, but it certainly gives peace of

mind." Stroking his moustache, he seemed pleased. He glanced at Emily, then Matt. "Do you want me to see if I can make some calls, maybe pull in some favors and get you some police protection?"

Mona's lips turned inward. "I guess it's better to be safe than sorry. If Emily really thinks she needs it, I suppose we should pay attention."

An angry looked flashed from under MacDonald's bushy gray eyebrows. "You make it sound like she's at fault, Mona." He had raised his voice, and seemed to have realized it, because he softened his tone and the anger disappeared. "Like you say, it's better to be safe than sorry."

Two red splotches appeared on Mona's cheeks. "Be careful, dear, your blood pressure." She put a hand on his arm. "Do you want coffee? Emily, could you put the coffee on?"

Emily left the room, and MacDonald looked at him, waiting for an answer to his question, so he said, "That's very kind of you, but I think we should be okay."

MacDonald raised his eyebrows. "Are you sure that's wise? Do have security training?" He twisted a gold Rolex on his wrist.

"We'll be okay," Matt said, getting the feeling that the judge wasn't the type of person who was used to being turned down. "But thank you."

Mona said, "I'm sure you will be. Emily always comes out all right in the end. I did my best, really I did, but it wasn't easy being a single mother. There were times when I struggled, but I think I did pretty well."

Sitting back, he said nothing, wondering if she really

thought this was true. Some things about Emily were beginning to make sense.

Conversation turned once more to home construction, but when Emily returned with coffee a few minutes later, Mona said, "Emily was always so dramatic." She added cream to a cup and handed it to Harold. "I remember once, she was three, I think, and she was locked in a closet. She was hysterical."

Emily steadied the coffee cup she'd just picked up with two hands. "How did that happen?"

Mona shrugged, turned to her daughter. "I don't remember. It was that closet under the stairs—we've since had it converted to a half bath—well, anyway, you started screaming." She took a sip of coffee. "Eventually, you fell asleep."

Emily said, "I've never heard that story before."

"Really?" Mona's tone was both surprised and pleased. She glanced at MacDonald, who cleared his throat and shifted in his seat.

"I recall the incident, but what I mean is that I haven't heard you tell the story before. I didn't realize it happened here."

"I would have thought you'd remember. You always did have a thing about being in tight spaces. But you've gotten over it, haven't you?"

Not answering, Emily gaped at her mother for a moment before putting down her cup. Standing, she turned to Matt. "Shall we go?"

Mona said, "I hope we'll see you both on Saturday." Her light tone suggested obliviousness to the unease in the air.

The judge rose, brightening. "It's Mona's fiftieth birthday. We're having a small get-together here, about twenty people, very casual. I wanted to have it at my place, but it isn't ready yet."

Emily was noncommittal. "I'm sure you'll have a very nice time."

Her mother said, "You have to come. You can't not come to my special day." She shot a glance at her boyfriend. "Harold has been working so hard that I've been feeling neglected."

Emily glanced at him, but Matt kept his face expressionless. It was up to her. "Perhaps for a few minutes," she said in a strained voice.

"Good, that's settled." Mona stood up. "I was hoping you could help in the kitchen. Most of the planning is done, but we could use an extra hand. It's going to be very low key, nothing formal."

He stiffened, a retort on the tip of his tongue but a look from Emily silenced him. She said, "Saturday? That's the day after tomorrow, isn't it? It's not very much time to prepare."

"Really, if it's too much to ask, just say so." Mona pressed her lips together. "I just thought we needed some happiness after what has happened to this family. Should I try to look for someone else?"

"That's okay." Emily's tone was remote, as if she was thinking about something else. "I can be an extra set of hands."

Mona's lips lifted into just a suggestion of a smile. "Good, we'll see you this weekend."

* * *

Emily grabbed a small plastic bag of clothes from the backseat of the rental car and followed Matt into a ground-floor room at the Prince Inn, the motel Matt had checked them into earlier. Five blocks north of the downtown core, it was sandwiched between a service station and an empty parking lot. Across the street stood a large grocery store.

Inside, a peculiar smell, as if somebody had tried to mask cigarette smoke with a heavy-duty odor remover, greeted her. Two double beds hogged the floor space. Emily walked to the farthest bed, tossed the bag on the flowery satin bedspread, and sat down.

"You didn't want more clothes?"

"That's all there was, aside from a winter coat." She shifted back on the bed, leaned against the headboard. "My mother must have gotten rid of the rest. She told me she was going to do it. She hates clutter."

"So I noticed." Smiling, he sat down on the other bed, facing her.

An attempt to return the smile failed. Her mind was full of an image of herself as a terrified little kid locked in a closet. It was an actual memory, not something she'd conjured up. She said, "I get so angry at her. Does that make me a bad person?"

"I think you have remarkable restraint."

A chuckle escaped her lips. "That's the sort of thing Amber would have said. She called me a world-class expert at tiptoeing around my mother. Amber said my mother gave me a role in our family. I was the misfit. As long as attention focused on what I did wrong, the real issues didn't have to be faced."

"And those issues were?"

"They've changed over the years, but I know she's very lonely. Which brings me to another point. She told me that she and the judge are getting married, although it's all very hush-hush."

He raised his eyebrows. "When is this happening?"

"She said she's waiting for this business with Amber to be over." Closing her eyes, she massaged her temples. "In other words, her happiness is being delayed because of me."

"That's pretty unfair."

"It's funny, I know she wants desperately to get married, but it's not a subject we could ever discuss. So in a way today was progress."

He watched her closely, eyes attentive. "The story your mother told about the closet, that was the first you'd heard of it?"

A big lump in her throat made it hard to speak. After a minute, she said, "When she said that, it all made sense. But I still don't know how I got in there." Looking straight ahead, aware of Matt in her peripheral vision, she said, "I'm not sure I really want to know, or that it even matters. But in a way, she had a point. I shouldn't have been screaming."

"You were three years old."

"Well, I should have gotten over it by now." She wiped a tear, waited a moment before she continued. "Don't get me wrong, I'm really angry at my mother. But I love her. I love her a lot."

"I can see that."

"I guess I've been stuck between being angry at her and loving her for a long time. You get numb after a while." He nodded and she continued. "I used to get angry and upset a lot. But it's safer when she doesn't know I'm mad. She can't mess with my head if she doesn't know what's going on inside it."

Matt opened his mouth to say something, but stopped. She really liked him for that, for not launching into a vicious attack on her mother. It felt good that he understood, and that he had defended her. That hadn't happened a lot. Everyone seemed to love her mother. They just saw the charming businesswoman. Amber was the other exception. Sometimes Emily thought she never would have survived her childhood intact if it hadn't been for Amber.

He said, "Do you want to cancel your kitchen duties for Saturday?"

"It's her birthday. If I have to go, I'd just as soon be in the kitchen. Her parties aren't my kind of thing, but I agreed because I thought we might be able to find something out. It'll give us another chance to talk to Celia."

"I can be your personal security detail, if that's all right."

She smiled. "I would feel a lot better."

"Better as in safer, or would you like to have me around?" A smile softened the question but his eyes smoldered with intensity and there seemed to be heat radiating off his body.

She let herself look at him for a long moment, her heart fluttering in her chest. "I'm not used to having anybody around, as you call it."

"You sound proud of that, like you're 'uncatchable.'"

"Shouldn't I be?" She put her head down, not sure she could control herself if she looked at him, and picked at a loose thread on the bedspread.

"Are you kidding me? It's not a crime, you know, to have someone."

"I know. I'm just used to taking care of myself. I've had to do it for a long time." Swallowing hard, she looked up. "And everything is so mixed up right now. It's hard to see past that."

Especially when it came to him. He wasn't even her type, but that calm, confident way he had about him, together with those rugged good looks, made her heart beat like a drum. When he touched her, kissed her, even held her hand, her body came alive. And the way he looked at her, with raw heat, as if nothing else mattered, he couldn't be faking that, could he?

He didn't say anything to that, just nodded. "Do you want to get something to eat?"

"I'm not hungry. But you go ahead." What she really wanted was to have a shower, then crawl in bed.

Preferably with you.

Feeling the heat rise in her cheeks, she looked away, thankful she hadn't said that out loud. "But you go ahead. I'll be fine here." If he left, she could try to get her raging feelings under control before it was too late.

"How about take-out?" When she nodded, he said, "I almost forgot. The pictures look too dark and far away to give us anything useful, but the guy said he'd see what he could do. He's got some sort of computer program that he'll run them through."

Emily frowned. "So where do we go from here?"

"You don't give up, do you?" He smiled. "Tomorrow, we'll go see the boyfriend. I don't want to call him to set something up. He might refuse to see us."

"We just show up?"

He nodded. "I found out where he lives. We'll see if we can get a feel for whether he's lying about that alibi."

"One other thing." Emily ran both hands through her hair. "My mother was right about my hair. I have to do something about it. I'll let the color grow out, but maybe the cut can be tidied up."

"Do you have somebody you normally go to?"

"I'd rather go somewhere they don't know me, where I won't get too many questions."

"We'll find something first thing in the morning. After that, we'll go see Jason."

Swinging her legs over the edge of the bed, she stood up. "I'm going to take a shower." Matt got to his feet at the same time and she found herself staring at his chest. Leaning forward, she rested the top of her head against him. He wrapped his arms around her, drawing her close. Turning her head to the side, she heard his heart thumping against his chest. Warm hands caressed her back and she felt herself get light-headed.

Releasing her, he picked up the car keys. "Pizza okay?"

When he'd gone, she walked to the bathroom and looked in the mirror. There was naked need in the flushed face, the shining eyes. But something else was imprinted there, an awareness that her feelings for Matt were much deeper than physical need. She shivered. It was almost as if she was looking at a stranger, someone who looked terribly exposed and vulnerable.

Like somebody who wasn't in control at all.

CHAPTER TEN

At ten the next morning, Matt was finishing up a cell phone call to his company in Boston when Emily came out of the hair salon. The ultrashort cut was one only a woman with her delicate features could pull off. He wanted to lean over, kiss her, but held back. She seemed to have put a wall between them.

"It suits you," he said, pulling away from the curb. Murmuring thanks, she looked ahead, not meeting his eyes. Earlier, at her bank, she'd withdrawn a wad of cash, insisting she would be paying for everything from here on in.

A few minutes later, they reached the street of postwar bungalows where Jason Hatt lived. A gray sports car was parked in the driveway beside his house. Matt drove by, parked down the street and they walked back.

"Nicky, my friend, grew up on this street, about two blocks down. I used to hang out there a lot. Her sister made a mean tuna casserole."

"Did your mother cook?"

"Never. She had a housekeeper for that and we ate at the hotel a lot."

Her tone was flat. He wanted to ask her about that but let it go. Now didn't seem the time to push it.

They got out of the car and walked up the sidewalk to Jason Hatt's house. He said, "You sound pretty tight with this Nicky."

She smiled. "She's a great friend. We're like night and day. I didn't talk to her much about this. I didn't want to drag her into it."

They reached the front step and she rang the doorbell. Seconds later, the door opened just wide enough for a man to put his head out.

Emily introduced herself. "Hi, I'm Emily Blackstock, Amber's cousin. Can we talk to you?"

He was easily six foot two, in his late thirties, with angry eyebrows that gave him permanent frown lines. "I've got nothing to say. Go away."

Emily stepped forward before he could shut the door. "We want to help."

The door opened farther. Scowling, he shot Matt a glance. "Help? How could you possibly help me?"

Emily didn't flinch, but Matt stepped closer. She said, "We want to find out who really killed Amber."

Jason's expression softened a degree, from outright menacing to merely surly. "I don't know anything."

She said, "Just talk to us. Any little thing that you could tell us might be useful."

Jason gestured to him. "Who's he?"

"He's a friend, Matt Herrington. He's helping me."

"Ten minutes, that's it." Jason opened the door and they stepped into a small foyer off the living room. He was wearing a navy-blue bathrobe and told them to sit in the living room while he got dressed. Jason returned in a couple of minutes, wearing jeans and a navy-blue polo shirt. He lowered his big frame into a swivel chair opposite the sofa where they were sitting and looked at Emily. "How can you possibly help me?"

"Do you think Amber killed herself?"

"Of course not. She had plans. She talked about going back to school with some of the money from her insurance payout. I don't believe it for a minute."

"Was she on drugs?"

"I know she wasn't—and I'm trained to look for that kind of thing."

"Did she tell you she was scared?"

He twirled a chunky gold ring with a red stone around his middle finger. "She was getting paranoid, making comments about the legal system, how corrupt it was." After a silence, he added, "We had a fight about it. I mean, it was like it was really personal. It was like an attack on all of us."

Emily said, "Us?"

"She said the whole system was corrupt." His anger seemed to have deflated, like air from a balloon, although he was still edgy, bouncing one of his knees up and down.

Emily sat forward. "What did she mean? The police?"

He shrugged his shoulders. "Look, I don't know anything. I already told you that. It maybe had something to do with the insurance thing. It kept getting delayed, but I don't know." Jason got up quickly. "You want anything to drink? Water?"

When they said no, he went off to the kitchen, came back a moment later with a bottle of water for himself.

Matt said, "What about your alibi? You were with another woman?"

Jason crossed his arms over his chest. "It was a woman, but not a girlfriend, if that's what you're thinking."

Emily said, "Who is she?"

"It doesn't matter. The police won't believe her. But I didn't kill Amber. I would never have done that." Matt said, "So who did?"

"I have no idea. But I think they're trying to set me up for it. They've got no evidence, but it doesn't matter. Everyone's buying it. You're the first people who've come here since the news about me broke. It's like I have a disease." He chugged back the water. "The funny thing is I could have avoided it."

Emily perked up. "What do you mean?"

"Why do you think they reopened the case?"

"It sounded like they wanted to cover all the bases and they found a problem with your alibi."

"Is that what they told you?" He shook his head in disgust. "I was the one who got it reopened." Matt sat forward, waited for Jason to explain.

"I was at court one day, ran into a reporter I know. We were talking about it. I told her it was fishy. She checked it out and got some pushback. The story went nowhere. Don't look so surprised. In a town like this, it happens all the time." He finished the water. "Listen, I don't know anything more. But there was nothing wrong with my alibi."

Emily said, "So why won't they accept it?"

He lowered his voice. "Because the woman who gave my alibi is an addict, that's why. She actually introduced me to Amber at a meeting. She hasn't done as well with staying clean and she's got a record for possession." He stood up. "I don't want to talk any more about her. I've said all I can say."

He walked them to the door, stood in the doorway as they stepped outside. "Talk to Celia."

Emily raised her eyebrows. "About what?"

"Amber kept going on about Celia trying to beat a DUI." He held up his hand to stop more questions. "Just be careful they don't come after you."

In the car, Matt swiveled in his seat so he was facing her side-on.

She said, "A lot of what he says backs up what I was saying. He didn't think Amber was back on drugs, either. My gut is still telling me he didn't kill Amber, but I also get the feeling he's holding back."

"He could be. But what? Who is this woman?" He put the key in the ignition. "We have to talk to Celia about this driving under the influence thing. Do you know anything about that?"

"First I've heard of it. But what could that have to do with Amber's death?"

Up the street, Jason came out of the house. He was wearing shorts and a sleeveless neon-green T-shirt. It wasn't the shirt that caught their attention, though. It was the tall blond woman who stepped out of the house behind him.

"So much for gut instinct." Emily's jaw had dropped. "I'd say that puts a whole different light on things."

He swore under his breath, watched Jason lock the door and set off with the woman down the sidewalk in the opposite direction. "We'll have to visit him again, see if he'll tell us the truth this time."

A fierce look darkened her eyes. "You'll have to put me in a straitjacket. Otherwise, I won't be held responsible for my actions."

"Don't give me ideas." He smiled but she gave him a hard look. Clearing his throat, he said, "In the meantime, I'm meeting the photography guy, his name is Bill Murphy, this afternoon. We can see if he found anything."

"Do you mind going alone? I should pop into the hotel, see what preparations have been made for my mother's party tomorrow. Supposedly, all I have to do is show up, but I'd like to be sure."

He rubbed the back of his neck. "I do mind, actually. I'd feel better if we stayed together."

Her response was a roll of her eyes. "Just drive. I'll be fine."

CHAPTER ELEVEN

Early the next afternoon, Matt surveyed the party-ready backyard at Mona Blackstock's house. If this was informal, he couldn't imagine what she considered formal. It looked like a setup for a fancy wedding, with four circular tables, each set for five people, arranged in the middle of the yard. They were covered in long white tablecloths, and crowded with plates, cutlery, and glasses.

Mona Blackstock and Celia Williams flitted from table to table, adjusting a plate here, a fork there, but not really doing much of anything that he could tell. Cold beer beckoned in a tub of ice on the ground next to a bar in front of thick shrubs at the back of the big yard. He'd wait until Mona and Celia cleared out. With no bartender yet, it might be against the rules.

In the house, a short hallway led to the kitchen. Emily, her hair tucked under a white cap and dressed in a white jacket, stood at a five-burner stove. She turned around to say something to a male chef working behind her at a granite-topped island in the middle of the kitchen, and they both laughed. Catching Matt looking, she smiled, turned back to the stove.

He walked over, leaned against the counter, and fingered the stiff fabric of her jacket sleeve, reached up and brushed her hair off her cheek. "How do you work in this? It looks like a straightjacket."

Smiling, she stirred something in a small frying pan. "There's beer in the fridge."

"You want one? It must be ten degrees hotter in here."

She took the pot off the burner and wiped her brow with a white bandana from her pocket, exposing the scar near her hairline. "Not allowed, I'm afraid."

The kitchen was big, but not big enough for three chefs and two waiters and a guy emptying a steamy dishwasher. The male chef couldn't keep his eyes off Emily but she didn't seem to notice.

Grabbing a beer from the fridge, he popped the cap, leaned against the counter, his elbows touching her arm. "If you have some of mine, I won't tell."

"I wouldn't dare. My mother has eyes on the back of her head." She poured the ingredients from the frying pan—some sort of herb in a vinegary-smelling liquid—into a mixing bowl and added mayonnaise and diced pickles.

"Who's he?" Matt gestured to the dishwasher guy, who was now scouring pots at the sink.

After a glance at the man, Emily turned and began slicing a bunch of green onions. "That's Junior, at least that's what we call him. I don't know his real name. He's worked for my mother at the hotel for a few years."

"Parolee?"

She stopped cutting, shot him a quizzical look. "What makes you say that?"

"He's got a tattoo of a spiderweb on his neck. That could mean he's been in prison."

Her eyes widened. "That explains a lot. He's got some sketchy friends." She added mustard, anchovy paste, and sliced green onions to the bowl. "But he's okay. Not too sociable, but he works hard."

Matt felt a tiny alarm bell go off in his head. He would have to keep an eye on Junior. He pointed to the bowl. "What is that?"

"Remoulade sauce, better known as tartar sauce. It's for the grilled salmon."

"You look like you're enjoying yourself."

"Most of the work has been done. I wasn't really needed. It's way crazier at the hotel." She gestured to the good-looking chef, who was giving instructions to another woman in a chef's uniform. "Joe told me I could slip out."

Finished with the sauce, Emily transferred it to a glass bowl and put it in the fridge. She turned around in time to catch him snatching a tiny tart from a tray on the end of the island. He popped it into his mouth, tasting crab. "I guess you know that the way to a man's heart is through his stomach."

"Joe made those."

"You have a way of ruining all the fun. Did I ever tell you that?"

Smiling, she leaned back against the counter. "Someday I'll make you some, how about that?"

"I thought you didn't like cooking," he said, leaning in close so they were touching.

"I didn't say that. It's being a chef in a restaurant that I don't like. You get tired of making the same thing, the long hours, not having a life."

A young woman appeared in the doorway and Emily gave a yelp of delight. "Nicky! I didn't know you were coming."

The woman, a tall, slim brunette who looked about Emily's age, gave Emily a big hug. After a minute, she stepped back and Emily introduced her.

Smiling, Nicky shook his hand before turning back to her friend. "I can't stay long. I'm doing an extra shift tonight, but I stopped by on the chance I would see you. Why haven't you come to see me?"

"I'm sorry," she said. "Things are kind of hectic."

She looked at him, then back at Emily. "I'll bet they are."

Emily's face reddened, and the three chatted for a few minutes, until Emily's mother appeared in the doorway, gave her daughter a look that was hard to read. Nicky pursed her lips, whispered, "I have to go. Call me, okay?" She smiled at Matt, then disappeared down the hallway.

Catching her mother watching, Emily shot him a look of mock guilt and pushed away from the counter. "I'd better start on the sherbet."

Mona's blond hair was scraped back so tightly into a bun on top of her head it looked like she'd had Botox. Either that or she was startled, although she didn't seem like the type who got startled easily. As the people in the room became aware of her presence, they lowered their voices.

After talking to the chef, her mother approached Emily, who was putting frozen raspberries and sugar in a blender. "Will the sherbet have enough time? It can't be too soft."

"It will be fine," Emily said plainly.

"I'm so glad you came, my dear. And Celia, too, I'm so glad she took the afternoon off." With that, Mona walked into the hallway, smoothed the skirt on her pale silk suit, and disappeared.

When she had finished making the sherbet, they stepped out of the kitchen and stood in the back doorway. He said, "Do you know any of these people?"

"Mostly they're old friends of my mother's, but I don't really know them." She chuckled. "I don't think you have to be too concerned about my safety, though. I think we could fight this group off. And the police chief is here."

Smiling, he brushed a stray hair back from her face, taken aback again by the delicate beauty that belied the steel within. "Depends what kind of weapon they have. And maybe somebody will get emboldened by booze."

Emily laughed. "You know that cliché about the aunt or uncle who always gets drunk at parties? Well, that never happens with my mother. Everybody knows they have to behave themselves or risk the wrath of Mona Blackstock. She even threw somebody out once." She tapped his chest with her index finger. "So you better behave yourself."

He caught the finger, held on to it for a long second, stared into those big eyes. "I consider myself forewarned."

People were scattered around the yard, talking in small groups. Mona was sitting on a brown rattan sofa on a flagstone patio near the back door, talking to a woman perched on the edge of the sofa beside her. The police chief sat in a chair opposite them.

"It's a Fantin-Latour. This is its fourth year," Mona told the woman, who was squeezed into a canary yellow dress. "It's named after the French painter. You may have seen his paintings at the Musée d'Orsay. It's lovely, but I didn't realize it would get so big. I may have to have it yanked out." The woman nodded knowingly.

Celia Williams was at the bar, talking to a middle-aged guy who kept glancing away, as if looking for an escape route. Nearby, the judge, sipping on red wine, was showing a middle-aged couple a picture from his wallet. They laughed about something as he put it away.

Emily said, "Let's go talk to Celia." At his skeptical look, she added, "Don't worry. She'll be on her best behavior." She took off her cap and jacket and hung them on a black iron hook in the hallway. She was wearing a white peasant blouse and a long, crinkly skirt that she'd retrieved from her mother's house earlier in the week. She looked more relaxed than he'd ever seen her and some of the color was back in her cheeks. For once, it didn't look like fear was eating away at her.

It took a couple of minutes to get to the bar, because Emily stopped several times to say hello to people and introduce Matt. When they reached Celia, she was talking to the same man and they waited until he had been dispatched before they stepped forward.

Emily asked Celia how her mother was doing.

"She's okay. I spoke to her this morning, briefly." Her eyes were cool and her manner distant. On her lips was the same lipstick she'd worn the other day, Dried Blood Red. A bit of it was smeared on one of her front teeth. "She needed time away, just with everything that's happening. I wish I could get away, but it's just too busy this time of year."

She turned to go, but Emily said, "I wanted to clear something up with you." Celia arched an eyebrow, immediately defensive. Emily said, "What do you know about the insurance settlement Amber was about to receive?"

"Not too much. I know she was looking forward to the payout. I think she might have been thinking about taking some courses. And now the insurance company won't pay until this case is wrapped up. Why do you ask?"

He asked, "Did Amber have any concerns about the settlement?"

"Not that I'm aware of."

Emily said, "One other thing. What happened to your driving under the influence charge?"

Paling, she pitched her reply low. "What are you talking about? What charge?"

Emily said, "Apparently, it was something Amber was concerned about."

"Somebody's spreading lies." Grabbing Emily's elbow, Celia steered her to the side. "And they'd better be careful. That's slanderous."

He stood beside Emily. "Did Amber talk to you about it?"

Recovering now, Celia's initial alarm was turning to anger.

"Of course not. There's nothing to it." The cell phone she was holding in her hand rang. Turning aside, she answered the call, listened for a minute before launching into a lecture on the risks of not acting quickly in a seller's market.

He doubted they would get much more out of her about the rumored charge. Her denial had been vehement, but he had expected that. Was it possible Jason Hatt had made it up to divert attention? There had to be a way to find out more about it.

When Celia hung up a minute later, she said, "I'm very busy these days, and I have to get Amber's house on the market. I'll have to stage it. That means packing up that bottle collection. I started last week, but I was rushing so much I broke one of them and cut myself." She showed them a small cut near her thumb.

Emily's mother approached, said to Emily, "You should get back in the kitchen. Lunch is about to be served." She turned to Matt. "I've put you next to Celia. She'll be good company."

He was sure for a moment that he had misunderstood, that Emily wasn't being banished to the kitchen, but Celia took his arm.

"I'll help in the kitchen," he said, looking at Emily. She would be there. That's where he wanted to be.

Celia tightened her hold on his arm. "Oh, no, you won't."

Emily smiled. "It's okay. I'll see you soon." She walked off, leaving him to think that somehow she'd got the better end of the deal.

* * *

Three hours later, with most of the guests and kitchen staff gone, Emily plopped down on the patio sofa and stretched out her legs. Matt sat down beside her, lifting her legs and putting them across his lap.

"How was dinner?" she said, trying to ignore the shiver of pleasure his touch brought. He smoothed her skirt over her knees, rested those big hands on her legs.

"The food was great, the company not so much." Leaning back, he hooked an arm over the sofa. "Celia spent most of the time trying to talk everybody at the table into buying what I gathered was her newest listing. She kept insisting it had good bones, which I took to mean it needed major renovations. By the time dessert came around, I was ready to buy it just to shut her up."

She chuckled. "Sounds like Celia. She's so much like my mother it's scary."

"The sherbet was good, by the way. Not too soft, not too firm. Just right. A highlight of the meal, in my opinion." A smile crinkled his eyes, and he caressed her legs. It made her dizzy, the feel of his fingers through the thin fabric of her skirt.

He was wearing a white shirt and tan chinos, and was clean-shaven, but that impression of primal power still radiated from him. Suddenly, she wished everyone would leave so that they could be alone. The urge to touch him was like a raw hunger. A moist heat between her legs intensified. Hands shaking, she sipped white wine from the glass in her hand.

Across the lawn, her mother chatted with Harold, who had his arm around her waist. After a minute, her mother went inside and the judge came over.

"Am I interrupting?"

Smiling, she swung her legs down to the ground and invited him to sit.

"How are you? Tired out?" he said.

"I'm fine. Did you enjoy the party?"

The judge pursed his lips together. "Not my thing, but if it makes your mother happy..."

She must have looked surprised, because he said, laughing, "Don't tell your mother. She'll put me out to the curb if she finds out I'm not one hundred percent gung ho on these sorts of things." He leaned in, whispered, "Too stuffy."

Looking at her, Matt said, "But the food was great."

She took another sip of wine. "I hope my mother thinks so."

MacDonald reached over, took her hand. "Don't worry about your mother. She can be hard to please, as you and I both know. But she is very proud of you and loves you dearly."

"Thank you." She had no idea if she believed that, but it was a nice try. Maybe she'd underestimated him and his ability to read her mother.

"I understand you're thinking about going back to law school," he said. "If you want to switch schools and need any references, I may be able to help."

"Thanks. I'll keep that in mind."

"And I want you both to come up and see the house. That's an order."

She said, "That would be great. Mother says the view is to die for. In a few days, I promise."

He stood up, put on a mock-serious face. "I'm holding you to that."

After he'd gone, she turned to Matt. "I always thought he was after mom for her money, but I may be wrong. He's growing on me."

"What made you think he's interested in your mother's money?"

"Just something Amber once said. She could read people."

"He seems decent." He grabbed a glass of beer from the low table in front of them, took a sip. "He must have some money if he's building a house."

"You're probably right. I bet those suits he wears don't come cheap, either."

They watched the judge join Celia and another woman who were seated at one of the circular tables.

He said, "But I will tell you one thing. He is enjoying himself. I would say these types of gatherings are very much his type of tea."

"You could be right."

He said, "I like your friend."

"Nicky's great, isn't she? I'll have to call her when this is all over."

"How do you know each other?"

"We met in high school, in chemistry class of all places. She was having a lot of troubles with her father—her mother'd disappeared—and we just clicked. Shared misery, I guess."

"What do you mean, disappeared?"

"When Nicky was five, her mother took off one day and was never seen again. She'd left a note. I think it really messed Nicky up for a long time—I'm talking years. Her father's a doctor and he put a lot of pressure on her and her sister to make something of themselves." She stroked the stem of her wine glass. "In Nicky's case, that pressure backfired. She ended up doing some time in juvenile detention."

"For what?"

"She had this stupid boyfriend and they stole a boat together. And crashed it."

"Yikes."

She bristled. "But I don't want you to get the wrong idea. She's gotten her act together now. She works with kids in trouble and she's very good at it." They talked about Nicky for a few minutes then he said, "Celia seemed to be a bit uncomfortable with the questions, don't you think?"

"I think she was lying about the DUI. But I can't see what it has to do with Amber's murder."

"What if Amber found out and threatened to reveal it?"

"You don't murder your sister over that, do you?" She took another sip of wine. "And other people must have known about it."

Matt frowned. "You're right. We know Jason did. There must be others."

"I'd like to know how much the insurance settlement is worth. Aunt June, Amber's mother, will probably inherit, but she's already loaded."

"What about Celia? She'll inherit eventually."

She said, "Celia is pretty motivated by money, I'll give you that, but I don't think it would be enough to kill her own sister."

Finishing the beer, he put the glass down on the table in front of him. "We have to find out more about the settlement.

Do you think Amber's personal papers are still in her house?"

"I don't have a key, and I don't think I can ask for one without a lot of questions."

He had a mischievous grin on his face.

She shot him a stern look and shook her head from side to side. "We can't break in, if that's what you're thinking. Amber had the place locked up pretty securely. I don't think your little course will help us there."

The grin widened. "We'll have to deceive the heavens to cross the ocean."

"What the heck does that mean?"

"It's an ancient Chinese military strategy. The idea is to hide your real goal with a fake goal, until the real goal is achieved."

She rolled her eyes, ignored the flutter in her belly that his playful mood ignited. "And this helps us get into Amber's house how?"

"Let's say we wanted to help Celia, who is very busy at this time of year, as you and I and everyone else at this party probably knows by now. We could offer to pack up the bottle collection."

Nodding, she looked over at Celia, who was still talking to the judge and the other woman. "We certainly wouldn't want her to risk further injury." She stood up. "I'll go tell her the good news, get that key."

CHAPTER TWELVE

Sitting in the parked car in Amber's driveway two hours later, Matt turned to Emily. "Sure you want to do this?"

"I haven't been here since she was murdered. I didn't realize it would be so hard." She spoke in a low monotone and her eyes were wet. "But I have a lot of good memories, too."

Not knowing what to say, her reached over and touched her shoulder.

She took a deep breath and opened the car door. "Let's do this."

The grass needed cutting, but the small yellow bungalow looked well kept. The front door, painted a bold eggplant, showed personality. At the front door, Emily riffled through six or seven pieces of mail from a box beside the door. Aside from a letter, it was all junk mail. She said, "Somebody must be picking up the mail. This doesn't strike me as a lot."

The front door opened onto a small foyer and beyond that a hallway. The air was stuffy. Slipping off his shoes, he stepped onto the hardwood floor. The kitchen was to the left, a cramped room with barely enough space for the circular table next to the window.

To the right was the living room, another small room, painted white but brightened with yellow and purple cushions on the sofa and chair. There wasn't much furniture but it looked fresh and inviting. On the wall to the left of the doorway stood the antique bottle collection, dozens of them in a variety of colors, shapes, and sizes arranged in a custom-built shelving unit bolted to the wall. A box on the floor held three bottles. More flattened boxes stood against the wall, along with a bag of packing peanuts.

"Beautiful, aren't they?" Emily pointed to one of the bottles on a middle shelf, an aqua flask embossed with a girl on a bicycle. "This one's my favorite."

Looking up, he pointed to an oval flask with a short stubby neck in a rich green color. "I like that one. The scroll work is nice, but the color does it for me." She turned to look at him, smiling. "Just like your eyes."

Her reply was an eye roll. "That sounds like a cheesy pickup line."

He smiled at her, but she didn't return it. He had a sense she was drawing back into herself again, although it could have been because this was the first time she'd been in Amber's house since her cousin's death.

"You can't blame a guy for trying," he said, realizing it was getting harder for him to keep a distance. Standing in front of him, her T-shirt hugged her body, emphasizing a small waist. The impulse to put his hands around her, to trace his hand along that gentle curve, overwhelmed him. Stepping back, he looked away. She had no idea of the fire burning in his belly.

She said, "Let's search for the papers first."

After putting the mail on the table in the kitchen, Emily led him down the hallway. The same hardwood in the living room, a golden oak, continued down the hallway into the bedrooms. "She used one of the bedrooms as an office. Probably the best place to start."

The office was tiny, barely one hundred square feet, with a single bed against one wall and a small desk with a modern chair and a white rollout filing cabinet tucked underneath. Two bookcases mounted on the wall above the desk held paperbacks. White sheers covered the windows.

He said, "When you said she was neat, you weren't exaggerating. I could take a few lessons from her."

"Messy, are you?" She switched on the overhead light.

"Certainly not this tidy. Or do you think Celia took away a lot of stuff?"

Emily shook her head. "Her house was always like this. Well, except for when she was having drug problems. Even then it was pretty neat." She pointed to the filing cabinet. "It shouldn't take long to search. I was wondering if she had a will, if that would tell us anything."

"It might, if there is one."

Emily pulled out the filing cabinet. Amber's neatness, not surprisingly, extended to her filing system. She riffled through two dozen files, arranged alphabetically, including banking, correspondence, medical bills and records, warranties, and witnesses. There was no separate file for her will.

She grabbed a file labeled "insurance," sat on the bed, and started sifting through the papers. Matt looked through the rest of the files, selected banking, and sat at the desk. After a few minutes, not seeing anything that jumped out at him, he picked a file marked "house and auto."

When he looked up a few minutes later, Emily had a puzzled look on her face.

He said, "See something?"

"There are a lot of letters, most from the same law firm. The last one was six weeks ago. I think she was close to getting her insurance money. It looks like it was over five million dollars."

He put down a letter he was reading. "That's a lot of money."

"But it's weird. There's a lot of stuff circled and she keeps writing 'notes' in the margins, but I don't see any notes here or any file marked 'notes.'"

He walked over and stood beside her, leaning in for a closer look. "Maybe she kept them somewhere else."

"But where? Another thing, the letters are arranged by date, newest first, but some of them are out of order. That's not like Amber."

"Do you think somebody looked through them?"

She shrugged. "Maybe."

He read through a few of the letters. "The lawyer's cut was thirty-four percent."

She put down the paper she was reading. "That's what, one point seven five million? A lot of money."

"It seems a little high, but it could be normal. Did she write any letters to the lawyer challenging him on that fee?"

"Not that I can see. But now that you mention it, I don't see copies of any letters she wrote, which is kind of weird considering she kept everything else. Wouldn't she have kept copies of her own letters?"

"You'd think. Maybe she was on to something, or she thought she was, and was scared enough to make a separate file. Any idea where she'd hide it?"

She thought for a minute. "She does…I mean, she did have a hiding place. After she was off the drugs, she confessed she'd had a place where she kept a stash." She frowned. "But I have no idea where it is."

"Here? In this house?" At her nod, he said, "It shouldn't be too hard to search."

They started with the office bedroom, searching under the bed and in the closet. A careful search turned up nothing in the closet but clothes, Christmas decorations, and two vacuum cleaners, a new stick model for cleaning hardwood floors and an older canister style in an avocado green for carpets.

A thorough search of the master bedroom and kitchen turned up empty. He offered to do the bathroom and found nothing. An hour later, after a search of the basement, they came back to the office and sat down on the bed.

He said, "Could she have had a safety deposit box?"

"I didn't see anything about one in the banking file, but maybe she did."

"What about her computer?"

"The police took it. I asked about it a couple of weeks ago."

He said, "We should check the attic." He walked into the hallway, where there was a square opening cut into the ceiling.

While Emily grabbed a flashlight from a kitchen drawer, he brought a chair, stood on it, and pushed up the piece of plywood covering the opening. It opened with a loud creak, as if it hadn't been used in years.

Putting the flashlight in his mouth, he grabbed the edges of the opening and pulled himself up. Sitting with his feet dangling down, he cast a careful eye around. There was nothing but soft bats of pink insulation.

Emily's voice came from below. "Anything?"

Putting the plywood back in place, he dropped down to the chair while Emily steadied it. "Nothing."

He said, "Maybe she has a trick hiding place, like a hollowed-out book or a hidden safe behind a picture."

"Could be. Now that I think about it, she did mention it was clever." She rolled her eyes. "Maybe too clever."

They tackled the books in a small bookshelf in the hallway next. Finding nothing, they started on the pictures on the walls. Half an hour later, after returning a painting to a wall in the living room, he sat down on the sofa. "If there is a place she kept stuff, I don't think it's in this house. We've been here for three hours."

Emily sighed and walked over to the bottle display. "We should pack these up." She stepped back suddenly, pointed to small shards of chunky amber glass on the floor in front of the shelf. "Must be from the bottle Celia broke. Looks like she swept up the big pieces and left the rest."

"I'll go get a vacuum. There are a couple in the office closet." He returned a minute later and plunked the old canister-style vacuum and separate carpet attachment on the floor.

When Emily saw it, she smiled. "I see you don't vacuum much. That's for carpet."

"You're right. I picked it because it reminds me of one my mom used to have." He bent down to pick the vacuum up. "I'll go get the other one."

"Wait. Why would she have a carpet vacuum?" She looked at him for a long moment.

He stared at her, not understanding.

Dropping to her knees, she opened the canister. A thick vanilla envelope had been stuffed into the top compartment, where extra attachments were usually kept. Holding the envelope, she jumped up, smiling.

He gave her a thumbs-up. "That's pretty clever, of both of you."

"It's not like Amber to have two vacuums, and especially one with a carpet attachment when she has no carpet."

Someone opened the door. Emily, eyes wide in alarm, slipped the envelope underneath a seat cushion on the sofa.

Celia walked into the living room. "Remind me to paint that door," she said, not greeting them. "Who paints their front door purple?" She plopped down on the sofa, leaning back. Underneath her was the envelope, but she didn't seem to notice.

Emily said, "Want to go to the kitchen for a cup of tea?"

Celia shook her head no. "Are you just getting started?"

He said, "It won't take too long."

She looked at Emily. "I forgot to say so earlier, but Amber left the bottle collection to you."

Emily's eyes widened. "Are you sure?"

"I wouldn't have wanted it anyway." She flicked her hand.

"I'd be happy to have it." Emily sat down beside her cousin. "Did Amber have a will?"

"Apparently she had it drawn up not too long ago. We didn't know anything about it. Mom inherits, but she gave half to that addictions place where she worked. I'm sure that will be put to good use." She rolled her eyes, indicating she thought the exact opposite was true. "Nothing to me, her sister, but whatever."

She stood up. "Got to go. Just wanted to let you know you can take the bottles. And make sure you get that key back to me."

* * *

That night, back at the motel room, lights on and curtains closed, Emily sat on her bed with Amber's papers spread out around her. There was a standard letter-size notebook, eighty pages, and a file folder with about several dozen sheets of loose paper. They'd also grabbed a handful of files from the office so they could take a better look at them.

She picked up the notebook, leaned against the headboard. "I'll start with the notebook."

Matt looked through the file folder they'd found in the vacuum. "I don't see a will."

She looked up. "Maybe she hadn't got a copy yet."

After half an hour, Matt said, "I don't see anything that jumps out at me. In fact, I think some of these pages must be duplicates of what I saw at her house. They look familiar. I'll start going through the files from her office again."

A while later, she put down the notebook and stretched her neck. A dull ache above her eyes signaled the start of a tension headache. "From what I can see so far, these notes are all about the insurance case. She made a lot of notes. It looks like every time she talked to her lawyer or someone at the insurance company, she wrote down the name, date, and details of the conversation." She rubbed her temples. "But for a neat person, I'd forgotten how messy her writing was. And she uses a lot of abbreviations."

"How often did she make a note?"

She looked back to the first page. "She started in February, just a few things at first, and the case was obviously already going on by then. At first it's once a week or so, and it's pretty routine, but then she starts writing more and more."

"Anything important?" Standing up, he laced his fingers and stretched his arms out above his head, palms outward. Dark, wavy hair fell across his forehead. Side on, it was obvious he had the chest and back muscles to fill out his broad frame. He was wearing the same shirt, which fit him in the shoulders but was too large in the waist. No man should look that good.

"Emily?" He was staring at her. "Find anything?"

Feeling her cheeks warm, she looked down, bought time by picking up the notebook. "It…it's hard to say if there's anything important in here for us. Most of it is pretty mundane, like this one from July 24, 'Got a call from Joel'—that's her lawyer—'and he says court mediator may be appointed.' It's pretty dry reading."

"Is there anything personal?"

"Doesn't look like it. How are you doing?"

"Nothing stands out yet. She did have a lot of medical expenses. Some of them were covered by insurance, some not, but nothing outrageous."

Matt sat down and they resumed looking at the papers. Still feeling flushed, she resolved to give her full attention to the notebook.

It was another half hour before something made her snap to attention. She looked at Matt. "This is interesting. I skipped to the end. There is a note about a will. She picked a different lawyer to draw it up, somebody in Albany."

"Does she say why?"

She shook her head. "Maybe she had a falling out with this Ackerman, the one who was looking after the settlement."

"Do you know anything about him?"

"No, other than that he refused to see me before, probably because of client confidentiality, although he never did say. Should we try again?"

"I doubt he'd want to reveal what the problem was, if there was one."

"You're right. But how will we find out what he was doing that Amber objected to?"

He shrugged. "We need some sort of evidence to suggest he was doing something wrong, but I'm not seeing that here."

"You're right. Maybe she just wanted to give another lawyer some business. Amber was like that."

Matt picked up his cell phone. "Let's google him." After a minute, he said, "He's with Scott, Cameron, and Daly lawyers. There's a short bio. He specializes in civil litigation, practiced law for twenty-five years in Riverton. There's a picture, looks about fifty."

He handed her the phone and she took a look at the photograph. She was about to hand back the phone when something occurred to her. She looked more closely. "He was at the party."

Matt glanced at the picture. "You could be right. If it's the same guy I'm thinking of, he was sitting one table over, next to a woman with long gray hair."

She nodded slowly. "Mrs. Ackerman, yes, she's been at the house before. She's quite stylish. He's short but a big guy, looks more like a body builder than a lawyer. He didn't stay long."

"You know, I think he might have left early. Maybe he was trying to avoid us."

She turned her attention back to the notes. There had to be more to the notes than she was seeing, if Amber had bothered to hide them. But what? "This is interesting," she said a few minutes later. "Amber wrote in mid-August—that would have been just before she was killed—about a phone call to her lawyer. She wrote, 'Called J. Ackerman to discuss issues with settlement. He said his secretary would call for a time.' Two days later, she writes, 'Still no word from lawyer. Jason says to be patient.'"

"Did she ever get that call?"

"No, I checked. I wonder what she wanted to talk to him about."

"It almost sounds like she thought he was avoiding her."

"That's another thing to ask Jason about. We know Amber talked about it with him. The lawyer won't tell us, but maybe Jason will."

"You're right." He stood up, stretched his arms. "There are still more pages, but my eyes are getting buggy. Want to take a break, go out for a beer?"

"Okay, just let me use the bathroom." She went in, pulled a comb through her hair, put on some lip gloss.

When she came out, Matt went in. She gathered up the papers and slipped them into the vanilla envelope.

A sound came from outside, a car door closing. She walked to the window, drew the curtain aside with a finger. Two men stood beside a car, looking in her direction. One of them was large, the same size as the man who had chased her at the cabin.

Heart pounding, she ran to the bathroom, tapped on the door. When it opened, she told Matt what she'd seen. His face went gray, and then he told her to grab the files and their shoes. While she did that, he picked up his multi-tool from his knapsack and something from a drawer in the desk and walked over to the locked door leading to the adjoining room.

"What are you doing?" she hissed. "We've got to go out the window."

He put his hands to his lips, whispered, "It's a tumbler lock, easy to open." He put one of the tools at the bottom of the lock.

Her knees went weak, threatened to give out. This couldn't be happening. "What if there are people in there?" Ears pricked, she thought she heard footsteps on the walkway outside their room, but her heart was beating so loudly she could have imagined it.

"I hope they don't mind guests."

Matt put a paperclip in the top of the lock and did something with the tool at the bottom of the lock. It clicked open.

She slipped into the room first, grabbing the knapsack. He pulled the door closed, locked it. She stood ramrod straight against the wall, not moving, not breathing, her pulse pounding in her throat.

Not a second later, the door to their old room opened.

CHAPTER THIRTEEN

Standing flat against the wall, Matt cast a quick eye around the adjoining room. With the curtains open, bright lights from the parking lot streamed down through the double-paned window across the floor, bouncing onto the walls and their faces.

Taking Emily's shaking hand, he pointed to the floor and they inched down. Only when he was sitting in the shadows did he dare release his breath. Putting his arm around Emily, he pulled her close.

The men were moving around in the other room, talking, not loudly but not whispering either. Putting his ear to the wall, he couldn't make out words. There was more shuffling. A minute later, there was a scrape of metals rings across a rod. One of them had opened the shower curtain.

Five minutes later, the men left the room and stood on the walkway outside the door, talking again. A moment later the acrid smell of cigarette smoke wafted in the air. The sliding window was open six inches. Emily stared at it, wide-eyed. He squeezed her hand.

The men walked to their car. He stayed where he was for a few minutes, just to be sure, before getting up. Picking up the files, he stuffed them into his knapsack. "We'll have to go out the bathroom window. They may be watching our room, waiting for us to come back."

"What about our stuff?"

"We'll have to leave it. It's too risky to go back."

He went through the window first, dropping onto the strip of mowed grass behind the motel, caught the knapsack Emily tossed down, and helped her to the ground.

They crept along the side of the motel to the far corner. At the front of the motel, across the street, the grocery store was closed but the large parking lot out front was illuminated. To the side was an empty parking lot. Behind them was an apartment building, separated by a six-foot-high chain-link fence. That was their best bet.

They climbed the fence, crossed the grounds of the apartment building, and kept moving, not stopping for ten minutes until they came to a school three blocks away. Streetlights cast a yellowish glow on a row of small houses opposite the school.

Emily let out a long breath before she chuckled. "So that's why you like old motels."

"What? Did you think it was the decor?" He smiled. "Stick with me. You'll learn a thing or two. Like the fact that old motels sometimes still have old locks."

"Please tell me that in your normal life you don't break into other people's motel rooms."

"Nope, just one of those skills that was useless until tonight." A dog barked from the backyard of one of the houses. "I'm going to go get another car."

"Can't we just get a cab?"

"I'd like to, but cab drivers tend to remember their passengers." Especially when they looked like she did. "Want to come or wait here?"

She glanced around, pointed at a covered side entrance of the school. "I'll wait there."

"I'll be back as soon as I can."

She touched his arm. "Try not to pick the most expensive car you see."

For a moment, he thought she was serious, but she smiled, lifting the corners of her mouth. Crinkles appeared around her eyes.

His heart did a funny flip. She'd never have to wear makeup, not with a smile like that. It made her the most beautiful woman in the world. It made him hate to leave her side, but he had to get a car.

Fifteen minutes later, he pulled up in an older-model white Chevy. Rolling down the window, he whistled and, as Emily ran up, leaned across and opened the door.

He said, "I don't think anybody will be missing this car for at least a day. The mailbox at the house I got it from was stuffed full. I'm guessing they're away."

Twenty minutes later, they stopped on a side street near another motel. Opening the trunk, he found a rag, ripped it in two, and they wiped the Chevy for fingerprints.

Five minutes after that, Emily came out of the motel office with a key for a room at the back. She had insisted on paying. He put the knapsack down on one of the two double beds, looked around at the fake wood paneling, worn carpet.

"No adjoining room," she said.

"We'll check out tomorrow."

"At least we know we have to be really careful." Shoulders drooping, she sat on the bed, staring at her hands.

He said, "Let's try to get some sleep. We'll go see Jason tomorrow. He's our best lead."

"He's our only lead," she said, her tone leaving no doubt that she wasn't banking on him having much to say.

* * *

Early the next morning, Emily waited at the motel room while Matt took a cab back to their old motel to pick up the rental car. They'd debated leaving it there, phoning the rental company to tell them where it was, but decided to take a chance and keep it. It would take too much time to get a new one.

She was wearing the clothes she'd slept in, but was long past caring. Rubbing puffy eyes, she tried to remember the last time she'd had a good sleep. There was too much going through her head and a very soft mattress hadn't helped. Not to mention she'd spent half the night wishing Matt would leave his bed and slip in beside her. She stole a peek out the window. The parking lot was empty. A long, jagged crack spread across the pavement like a lightning bolt.

When Matt pulled in, she left the key on the desk in the room and got in the car. He put his hand to his mouth to stifle a big yawn.

The drive across town to Jason's house took twenty minutes, including a stop for take-out coffee and a muffin. His car wasn't in the driveway, but she rang the doorbell anyway to confirm he wasn't there.

"I wonder where he is," Matt said when she got back in the car.

She thought about it. "Didn't he say something about either being at home or at the gym?"

"We drove by one. It's just a couple of blocks away." He started the car. "Let's check."

His car wasn't in the lot of the fitness club near his house, but they decided to check another, bigger club farther down the street. Driving by a few minutes later, they spied Jason's silver sports car at the rear of the parking lot. Matt parked at a meter on the street, and they walked back, sat on a bus bench with a clear view of the rear entrance of the club across the street.

It was forty minutes before Jason came out, and he was halfway to his car when they caught up with him.

He threw his hands up in the air when he saw them. "Stay away from me."

She said, "Answer one question, and we'll leave you alone."

"What?"

She walked closer. "We found some notes of Amber's. She made a reference to a problem she was having with her lawyer."

"Yeah, and…"

"What was the problem? Did she think the settlement was not enough money?"

He snorted. "Are you kidding? She actually thought the settlement was too much, if you can believe it. But she was frustrated because it was dragging on."

She said, "Why was that?"

"The lawyer was trying to get more money, threatening to go to trial." He backed up toward his car. "Listen, if you know what's good for you, you'll drop this whole thing."

As he turned toward his car, she called out, "Did Amber find out about your girlfriend?"

Turning around, Jason looked at her, not understanding.

"We saw you with her the other day, leaving your house."

"Is that what you think of me?" He glared at her. "That was my sister."

"You have a sister?"

"I'm trying to help her through a rough patch. She's my alibi, but the cops won't believe her because she's an addict and they think she's lying because she's my sister."

"Why didn't you tell us?"

"Why do you think?" He cursed. "Riverton's a small town. She doesn't want everyone to know." His face had flushed an angry red and he started moving toward her. "Besides, it's none of your damn business."

Matt put himself between them, told her to go.

"I'm sorry." Stomach cramping, she stumbled back.

Matt released Jason, who stalked off toward his car. He waited until Jason was close to the car before he turned and started walking toward her, looking at the ground, avoiding her eyes.

Way to go, Emily. Way to eff things up.

A second later, there was a boom, a hollow, deafening sound. At the same time, a wave of pressure hit every part of her body with the force of a knockout punch, slamming her into the ground.

Sprawled face-down on the pavement, she lay stunned for a moment, breathless, the pavement spinning around her. It was hard to hear. For some reason her ears were plugged, like on an airplane when you're waiting for them to pop. A pungent smell, maybe gunpowder, burned her lungs. Gunpowder? What was happening?

Lifting her head, her eyes caught pieces of a car mirror strewn on the pavement. Behind her, a yellow-orange fireball and plumes of thick, black smoke shot high in the air.

Oh, God.

Behind her, a bald man with bulging eyes was shouting into a cell phone, his voice muffled as if it were coming from a long way away. A car battery had exploded, he yelled. People were dead.

She tried to lift her head but it felt as heavy as a bag of sand.

Matt. Where was Matt?

A woman rushed to her side. "Stay still. You're going to be okay." Kneeling down, she blocked Emily's view of Matt and the burning wreckage.

Emily tried to get up but the woman held her down. "It's best not to move." Lifting her head, she barked an order at the people standing in front of them. "Someone get me some blankets. Now."

Tears bursting from the corners of her eyes, Emily grabbed

the woman's hand. "I was with a man, a tall man. His name's Matt. What happened to him?"

The woman glanced behind her across the pavement. Turning back, blue eyes avoided Emily's. "Don't think about that right now. Help is coming and you're going to be all right."

A searing pain gripped her heart, tore it into pieces.

CHAPTER FOURTEEN

Hot pavement scorched Emily's skin. Strange, then, that she should feel cold, her skin clammy, teeth chattering. The smell of smoke and burning rubber burned her throat. People stood watching, bewildered. A fleshy-faced man came with a blanket and spoke to the woman taking care of her. His voice was muted by the sound of somebody moaning.

Matt is dead.

She didn't want to move. Better to die right there. But she had to see him. It was her fault. She owed him that much. Using her elbows, she tried to get up. The woman held her back but Emily cursed loudly, shoved her hand away, and sat up. Realized, dimly, that the person moaning had been herself.

A man with a portable fire extinguisher sprayed white foam at Jason's blackened car. The roof had blown off and teetered upside down on the hood of the car beside it. The bald man was still on the cell phone, not yelling now but pacing back and forth. In front of her, two men dragged the limp body of a man across the pavement away from the burning wreckage.

Matt.

Stumbling to her feet, she staggered forward, smashed glass crunching underfoot. As the men laid Matt on the pavement, she dropped beside him. His eyes were open and his face was contorted in pain. "You okay?" he choked out.

Tears welled up in her eyes, started running down her cheeks. Choking back a sob, she nodded, ran a cursory glance over him. His right forearm was bleeding from a cut, but there were no major wounds that she could see. A layer of dust coated his hair gray, and there was a smear of what looked like grease on his chin.

"Where are you hurt?" A flood of emotions uncoiled deep inside her, a jumble of anger, fear, guilt. She was responsible for this.

He grimaced. "I think I broke my arm, but I'm okay. Jason?"

Wiping away tears, she shook her head. The light dulled in his eyes.

Oh, God, what have I done? Jason was dead. Matt had escaped, but barely.

Confused people shouted around them, their voices mixing with the wail of sirens in the distance. A police car screeched to a stop at a haphazard angle in the parking lot. The siren stopped, but there was another one, higher pitched, and moments later an ambulance pulled alongside. More police cruisers arrived and officers started clearing people from the parking lot.

She stepped back while the paramedics attending to Matt put him on a stretcher and wheeled him into the ambulance.

Climbing in beside him, she hung her head in her hands.

He reached over and touched her arm. "This is not your fault."

Rocking back and forth, she flinched as the ambulance doors shut. Of course it was her fault. The tears refused to slow.

The ambulance driver left the siren off on the way to the hospital. Ashen faced, Matt clenched his teeth. At the hospital, a doctor ordered intravenous pain medication and an x-ray.

A uniformed police officer appeared in the doorway and asked her to come out. They walked to a vacant examining room, where the detective she'd talked to with Matt, Sam Fisher, was waiting. For the next hour, he grilled her about what happened while the uniformed officer took notes. No, she hadn't seen anything suspicious. No, she didn't have any specific information about why Jason Hatt was targeted. When Fisher moved on to questions about Amber, she cursed under breath. There was nothing new she could tell him.

When they let her go, the door to Matt's examining room was closed so she walked out to the waiting area and found an empty chair against the back wall. A bored-looking man with a paunch stared at her, as if trying to guess her ailment, but she gave him a hard stare and he turned his attention back to a weather report on the television.

She couldn't think clearly, the thoughts in her head twisting like a ball of yarn—except for one clarifying thought. The search for Amber's killer was futile. Talking to the cops—seeing their unbelieving looks—was enough to make her realize that. Never mind that it had led to Jason's murder.

An awful hollowness filled her chest. Matt had been right

when he'd accused her of being stubborn. Why hadn't she listened to him?

An hour later, Matt appeared, looking pale, his arm in a cast.

She rose to greet him, fingered the cloth sling supporting his arm. "How are you?"

"I broke two bones in my forearm. They drugged me up with something, so I'm not thinking too clearly right now. Other than that I'm okay."

He swayed slightly and she moved around to his left side and put an arm around him. Dark shadows under his eyes signaled his tiredness. He gave an impression of vulnerability that made him unbearably attractive. Her heart skipping, she fought the urge to reach out and touch him.

She said, "The police want to talk to you."

"Later. Right now, I'd feel safer if we got out of sight. Let's get a cab back to the rental car. After that, we can figure out what to do."

In the fifteen-minute cab ride to their car, it didn't look like anyone was following them, but she couldn't be sure. She snatched two parking tickets out from under the windshield wiper, then drove down the street to a hotel, the Belvedere, where they checked into a room on the second floor. Inside the room, Matt lay down on the bed without going under the covers, closed his eyes. After a few minutes, his breathing slowed and he was asleep.

Opening a set of sliding doors to a small concrete patio, she stepped out, looked out at the parking lot. An image of Matt lying on the pavement, thick smoke behind him, was playing on a continuous loop in her brain. She had been sure he was dead. Tears forming in her eyes, she took a couple of deep breaths. *Hold it together. Let him sleep. We'll figure out what to do.*

Behind her, the sliding door scraped open. Flinching, she whirled around.

Matt stepped onto the small balcony. "It's just me. I didn't mean to scare you." Standing beside her, he squeezed her shoulder. "Are you okay?"

Wiping clammy hands on her shorts, she took in the wrinkled brow, the expectant look in his eyes as he waited for an answer. She'd almost gotten him killed and he was worried about *her*?

She had to get away from him, to get out of his life. "Do you want me to get you some pain medication? There's a drugstore down the street."

"I'm okay for a while." He smiled reassuringly.

Crossing her arms, she faced him square-on. "This is over, Matt. I can't do this anymore."

He looked at her blankly. "What do you mean?"

"Jason's dead." She swallowed, the fear she felt for him rising like bile in her throat. "You were almost killed."

Mouth slackening, he shook his head. "We can't quit now. Jason's death is even more reason to go on."

She stared at him hard. "What if you were the target? When I was waiting for you at the hospital I couldn't get that idea out of my head."

"Jason was the target. The bomb was likely set to go off when he put the key in the ignition. Whoever did it wouldn't have known we were going to be there."

"Oh, God." She rubbed her face. "This is senseless."

He was silent.

"Will they be able to tell who made it?"

He shrugged. "I'm not sure. It was likely a pipe bomb. They're pretty easy to make. I'm guessing there won't be fingerprints."

No surprise there. His answer underlined the futility of their quest. Resolve hardened in her chest. "So we're no further ahead now than when we came to Riverton."

"We can eliminate Jason as our main suspect."

Disbelief had her shaking her head. "We can only eliminate suspects when they're killed off? That's pathetic." She pinched her lips together. "Don't you see? It's not worth it. I can't risk putting your life in more danger."

Tilting his head, he looked her in the eye, his expression tight. "Emily, you'll never be free unless we get to the bottom of this."

"That was before this happened. Why can't you see that?" Her words brought no change in his expression.

A black car pulled into the parking lot. Instantly, they backed up against the wall, watched as the driver found a spot near the road. A woman got out and took four or five shopping bags out of the trunk.

Letting out a breath, Emily looked at Matt, her eyes examining his face, the wide forehead, chiseled cheekbones, full lips, strong jaw, until at last they stopped at those dark eyes. Hot tears rolled down her cheeks. She had to do whatever it took to keep him safe. Even if that meant never seeing him again. Even if it felt like part of her would be torn away.

She wished she'd never met him. But it wasn't too late. The self-talk that came next was as familiar as a mantra. *You can handle this. You can get back in control. You are better on your own.* Repeat forty times.

When she spoke, her voice sounded flat, distant to her ears. "I'll go into hiding. I'll disappear. Forever if I have to."

He opened his mouth to speak but stopped himself, as if he knew she was right. Pivoting, he opened the door slowly, stepped inside.

She had expected anger, had even braced for a fight, but somehow his calm manner hurt more. Her face wet, vision blurring, she couldn't see him through the glass door. It was as if a thin, dark veil had been dragged like a curtain between them.

* * *

Matt slammed his fist into the bathroom door. Emily was right, of course. She had to go into hiding. That was the only way she could be safe.

Walking over to the sink, he turned on the faucet, used his left hand to splash icy water on his face. A hollowness burned in his chest. Straightening, he dried his face with a hand towel.

When he came out of the bathroom, Emily was sitting on the end of her bed. Heart hammering in his chest, he said, "Are you sure that's what you want to do?"

"Yes." She stared down at her hands and when she spoke her voice was flat. "It'll help if you give me some pointers, but I think I can do it on my own." She looked up, hopeful. "What are you going to do?"

Closing his eyes, he pinched his nose. "I still have to find out who's behind all this."

Standing up, she stared at him. "What? Why?"

"If I don't find out, I'd have to disappear, too." He took a breath. "I can't do that. I can't just leave everything, my company…"

She shuffled back a few steps.

Her swallowed hard. "Did you think I would come with you?"

Red blotches appeared on her face. "Of course not. I thought you would go back to Boston."

"They know who I am. They'll find me."

She leaned against the wall and sank slowly to the floor, covering her face with both hands.

He knelt in front of her and put a hand on her knee.

When she spoke her voice was a hoarse whisper. "I am so sorry. Never in a million years did I expect this to happen."

He wiped a tear from her cheek. "I know that. It's not your fault."

For some reason, it wasn't the right thing to say because she started sobbing uncontrollably. He shifted to her right side, put his arm around her, and pulled her close, stroked her hair with his left hand.

He said, "We've got to find somewhere safe for you to hide out." There was another reason for doing that. It was bad enough spending night after night in motel rooms trying to keep a distance. Now, despite the mounting danger, all he could think about was getting her in bed. That could get them both killed.

Her head jerked back and she looked at him with watery eyes. "What do you mean? I'm not going to hide out."

It was his turn to be surprised. "You just said you would."

Breaking away, she jumped to her feet. "That was when I thought you were leaving. Since you're not, I'm hardly going to go hide out. Whatever happened to being in this together?"

He stood up. "I'm not saying we're finished. You don't have to hide out forever, depending on what happens." The thought of her being in any more danger nauseated him.

"You are such a jerk." She glared at him a moment before turning to the door.

He caught her hand. "Where are you going?"

"For a walk. I have to get out of here."

He shook his head in disbelief. "Am I missing something here? I just don't want you to get hurt."

"And it's okay if you do?" She pulled her hand away, rubbed her wrists. "How does that make sense?"

"You're right, it doesn't. I just feel protective of you."

"You don't think I can look after myself, is that it?" Eyes lit with anger, she turned toward the door again.

Scratching the back of his head, he studied her. "So now you're going to go? Is that it? Just walk out?"

"It was a mistake, right from the start, trusting you. Letting you get close."

He scoffed. "You haven't let me get close. You've done everything you could not to let me get close."

He had hit a nerve. She froze, seemed to be trying to think of something to say.

He pushed. "Why is that?"

"Why are you making this my fault?" She crossed her arms over her chest.

"You're avoiding the question. Why won't you let me get close?"

"This is hardly the time to be having this discussion."

"You want to get close. I can see it."

She looked down, not saying anything. He waited, let the silence stretch between them. When she looked up, all traces of anger had vanished, replaced not by that cool and collected game face he'd expected, but by a look so raw and unfiltered his heart clenched.

She said, "Because if you get too close, you're not going to like what you see." Her eyes, deep and vulnerable, burned holes into him.

Walking over, he took her hand, recognizing the courage it took for her—especially for her—to expose that vulnerability. "It's the opposite. The closer I get, the more I like what I see."

She stood frozen in place, her eyes glassy with unshed tears.

He said, "I think you're the smartest, gutsiest, most beautiful woman I've ever met. What's not to like? Never mind that I can barely keep my hands off you." She stood, open-mouthed, not seeming to believe him, unidentifiable emotions flashing across her face. He said, "Tell me what you're thinking."

She said, with a kind of desperation, "You know, the usual, what a mess I've made of everything."

Tilting his head, he looked at her closely. "Did you ever think it might be the other way around, that things have made a mess of you?"

Her moist, expressive eyes looked huge in that pale face. "I think that's just about the nicest thing anyone has ever said to me."

He smirked. "Really? It wasn't *that* nice." The soft swell of her breasts was clearly visible under her T-shirt. He clenched his fists to stop himself from reaching for her.

She said, "It's funny what you said about having trouble keeping your hands off me." Something new and dark lit those eyes.

"Why is that funny?" he said, throat dry.

"I was thinking the same thing about you." She wet her lips, and reached up to stroke his cheek with long, pale fingers.

Her touch sent a surge of blood racing to his groin. Standing on her toes, she brought her lips to his. He shouldn't, he knew that, but couldn't stop himself. He'd waited too long. Sucking in a breath, he kissed those warm, soft lips, wanting to go slowly, taste every inch. His hand stroked the silky white skin of her neck.

Tentative at first, she put her arms around his neck and drew him close, swirling her tongue in his mouth and pressing herself against him. She was hurrying, trembling fingers struggling with the button of his jean shorts.

Pulling away, he looked into those gorgeous smoldering eyes. "Emily…"

Her hand went to her lips and she stumbled back. "Is something wrong? Did I do something wrong?"

He shook his head. "Are you sure you want to do this? No regrets?"

She was breathing heavily, the soft swell of her breasts rising and falling through the T-shirt. "No regrets."

"Okay, not too fast."

"Oh, God, I'm sorry." Blood rose in her cheeks and she pulled her arms tightly across her chest. "I'm nervous, I-I'm out of practice."

"It's okay."

She backed away and a hot flush crept up her neck. "Well, I can't really say that I'm out of practice, because that makes it sound like at some point I was in practice. And that is clearly not the case."

"I don't want somebody practiced. I want you, Emily. I knew the moment I first saw you, I wanted you. But I don't want quick and dirty, not this time. I want every square inch of you."

Chest heaving, she stared at him.

He sat on the bed and held a hand out to her. "Come here."

Taking his hand, she stood between his legs, looking down. Tilting his head up, he put his mouth on hers, felt her soft, moist breath. Nibbling her lips, she gave a little whimper as his tongue found hers.

Running his fingers through her hair, the kiss deepened. As she sucked gently on his tongue, he felt his erection pushing against his fly.

"Take off your shirt," he said in a gruff voice.

Pulling back, she lifted her T-shirt over her neck, stood before him in a white bra, a lacy thing with a pink bow in the middle. He traced his finger down her neck to the soft mound of a breast. A low moan escaped her throat and she arched her head back. Leaning in, he pulled down the fabric of the bra and thumbed her hard, pink nipple as more moans escaped her lips.

After a minute, he took off his shirt, and she unhooked her bra, exposing firm, round breasts. Those innocent eyes on him, she put her palms against his chest, drew wide circles. He left a trail of kisses on her breast until his mouth found a stiff nipple and began sucking it. After a long moment, he shifted back on the bed. Still sitting up, he drew her onto his lap, her knees on either side of him.

A sound came from the hallway outside. They froze, turned to listen as somebody entered the next room. The television came on.

He looked at Emily and smiled.

Still feeling shy, she said, "Can we get under the covers?"

She shifted off him and he stood up, reached over, and pulled back the sheets. "You get in first. I want to be on this side, because of my arm."

He slipped in beside her and put his arm under her head. She moved closer, so that she was on her side, facing him. Her eyes had flecks of brown and blue amid the green.

Molding her body to his, she wrapped her arms around his neck. His rough hand followed the curve of her waist down to the soft slope of her hip. Blood rushed through him and the need to be inside her was like an ache. He wondered how in the hell he was going to take this slowly.

CHAPTER FIFTEEN

Emily lay curled up in bed, her mind floating on a blissful cloud, her body sore in all the right places. Matt was talking on a cell phone on the balcony, but the door was closed and she couldn't hear him. He must have had a shower, because his hair was wet and tousled and he had a white towel wrapped around his waist.

The bedside clock said it was after nine. Shadowy morning light filtered in the west-facing window. She hadn't slept that well for weeks. Who knew sex could be like that, so intense physically and emotionally? Remembering her legs wrapped around that waist, the feel of him sleek and hard inside her, heat rose under her skin and she felt herself become wet.

Whew.

She got out of bed, crept into the bathroom, and turned on the shower. When she came out, wearing a bathrobe, he was still on the phone.

Five minutes later, finished with the cell phone call, he came back in the room, walked over and kissed her.

"How long have you been awake?" she said, reaching over to brush hair off his face.

"A couple of hours." Worry edged his voice and he seemed distracted.

"What's wrong? Who were you talking to on the phone?"

"My sister," he muttered. "My father's in the hospital."

Her heart caught. "Is he okay?"

"I think so, for now at least. He has really bad stomach pain and some sort of obstruction. They're trying to figure out whether he needs surgery or not. She doesn't really know much more than that right now."

A queasy feeling rose in her stomach. "You should go."

"She's going to give me a call later, when she knows more. As it stands right now, I don't think I have to go, at least not right away." He ran a hand through his hair.

She said, "I'll be okay."

He shook his head. "I'm not leaving. I can't anyway, at least until I talk to the police. They're expecting me in two hours."

She backed away. "How is your arm?"

"I should get something for it, take the edge off." He sat down on the bed. "I was talking to a friend from home who works for the *Boston Globe*. She called someone she knew at the Riverton paper, a reporter. He checked the court records here to see if there was anything on Celia. Apparently he's got good contacts, people who let him know stuff, but they couldn't find anything."

"Maybe there was no such thing. Maybe Jason was wrong,

or was lying. Maybe it has nothing to do with what happened to Amber anyway." Sitting down on the other bed, across from him, she fidgeted with the bedspread, tried to rein in a mounting feel of hopelessness.

He lifted the bedside phone. "Let me order some breakfast from room service. We can take another look at Amber's notes. Something Jason said is eating away at the back of my mind. I just can't put my finger on what it was."

"Just let me run out and get you some pain relievers."

"That's okay, it's not that bad."

While he phoned room service, she grabbed her clothes and went into the bathroom and changed. When she came out, Matt had changed into shorts and a T-shirt and was sitting on the bed looking at the notes.

She didn't know what it was—his father's illness, pain from his broken arm, or frustration with the investigation, maybe a combination of the three—but he seemed preoccupied and distant. His life had been turned upside down, all because of her. Was he questioning whether it was worth it? She likely would be, if she were in his position. A couple of hours of hot sex wouldn't change that.

Her heart shivered, the blissful peace she had felt half an hour earlier gone, leaving in its place something cold and forlorn.

There was a sound in the hallway outside their door. She darted a glance at Matt.

He said, "Probably just room service. I told them to leave the food outside."

It was room service. They tucked into omelets and coffee.

After, sitting on the bed with a second cup of coffee, she picked up Amber's notebook again. There were some pages she hadn't even looked at yet. Instead of feeling sorry for herself, she should be getting back to business.

She said, "Jason said something about Amber thinking she was getting too much money in the settlement."

Matt looked up, brows furrowed. "Now that you mention it, he did, didn't he? Most people don't complain about that sort of thing. And didn't Celia say she gave half of it in her will to the place she worked at?"

She nodded. "So Jason was right about that. But I can't see why somebody would kill her for complaining that the settlement was too much money."

"We have to get that lawyer, Ackerman, to talk to us. Maybe we should drop by his office, after I get back from talking to the cops."

He put down his coffee cup. "I'm going to slip out and get us some clothes. Any preferences? I'll be back within half an hour. Put the chain on the door when I've gone, okay?"

Smiling, he leaned down to kiss her on the lips. But there were tight lines around the corners of his mouth, and he still looked distracted, as if he'd already moved on.

* * *

Matt opened the bottle of Tylenol, popped two in his mouth, and took a long swig of water. Emily, who had let him back into the hotel room a minute earlier, was giving her full attention to the papers fanned out across the bed in front of her.

"How are you doing?" he said.

"These notes are starting to get easier to read. She writes in a kind of shorthand."

"I noticed that this morning," he said. "I took a look while you were still sleeping. She seems to have an aversion to vowels."

"Maybe she was worried about somebody getting their hands on them."

He gestured to the bag. "There are clothes in there for you."

She smiled, reached into the bag, and grabbed her clothes, disappeared into the bathroom to change. He wanted to stop her, kiss her, but she was too quick.

Rubbing his temples, he tried to think. His father's illness was way worse than he'd let on to Emily. Surgery sounded like a very real possibility. If it went ahead, he had to go home. But how the hell was he going to keep her safe in the meantime?

After she was done in the bathroom, he shaved and changed. When he came out, Emily looked up. "On July 12, that's, um, less than two weeks before she was murdered, Amber said she was worried about the lawyer representing her in the insurance case. She said she didn't trust him."

He sat down. "Does she say why?" When Emily shook her head, he said, "I wonder what that was all about. What would you do if you didn't trust your lawyer?"

She thought about it. "Go the law society? The police?"

A call came in on Matt's cell phone. He listened, took notes, and when he was done, she looked at him expectantly.

"That was the reporter in Riverton. There was a driving under the influence incident involving Celia. He talked to a cop friend." He referred to his notes. "It happened on June 11, a Friday evening. There was a call from dispatch about a car weaving all the road, heading north on Highway 11."

Emily said, "That's the main road going north-south outside of town."

He looked back at his notes. "Anyway, the cop found the car still running and pulled her over. She refused to take a sobriety test, but he smelled alcohol on her and suspected she was drunk. But she was never charged."

"Did the cop follow it up?"

"Yeah, and he was told to shut up. He didn't push it."

She furrowed her brows. "I still don't understand how this could relate to Amber's murder." She stood up suddenly. "I wonder who Celia's lawyer was. You think it could be this Ackerman character?"

"Good question. We should find out." He checked his watch. "I have to go see the police. I'd better call a cab. I shouldn't be driving with this cast."

"I'll stay here. I'm on a roll with these notes. If I keep at it, I should be done in an hour. Don't worry, I'll put the chain on the door."

"Keep that phone on. I'll call you and let you know how I'm doing."

After a nod, she dipped her head back to the notes.

CHAPTER SIXTEEN

For the first time since Amber had been murdered, Emily had the feeling that identifying the killer was within reach. It all seemed to come back to Amber's lawyer, Joel Ackerman. The lawyer had done something questionable. Amber had talked to Jason about it, but he had been too scared to tell her and Matt what it was.

Matt's question came back to mind: What would she do if there was a problem? She hadn't thought of it at the time, but she would go to MacDonald, of course. Obviously, Amber hadn't, because the judge would have told her if she had. But maybe the judge could find out if Amber had approached the judge in her case.

She had to talk to Harold. Standing up, she stretched. She could call her mother and ask for Harold's phone number, but her mother might object. She decided to walk to the courthouse, which was about ten minutes away. She wanted to get out of this room, anyway. Grabbing the cell phone and her notes, she took the Do Not Disturb sign off the door and left.

Outside, the day was warming up. It was too early for lunch, so the downtown sidewalks were mostly empty, except for a handful of shoppers who stopped to gaze inside boutique windows or inspect outdoor sales racks.

The courthouse was an imposing stone building, built more than a century earlier in a neoclassical style, with a wide Greek portico and four columns spaced evenly along the front. After passing through a security scanner, she approached the reception desk, explained who she was, and asked if Judge Harold MacDonald was available. Told to wait, she sat on a bench and called Matt on his cell phone. There was no answer and she wasn't given the option of leaving a message. No surprise there, considering the police interview was likely just beginning.

Five minutes later, the judge came down, escorted her up the balustrade steps to his chambers, a large room with dark wainscoting and one window that overlooked a side street. Taking off his robe, he hung it on a hook behind the oak door and gestured to a chair.

"It's lovely to see you. Sit down. Sit down. I just wrapped up a preliminary hearing, so I'm finished for the day. Did you come about the house?"

"The house?"

"You said you wanted a tour of the house." He sat down, facing her across a large metal desk.

"No, I'm sorry. I didn't."

He seemed taken aback, so she said, "But I'd love to have a tour. It's just that right now I need your advice." She took a minute to explain and showed him Amber's notes.

He looked at the notes, brows furrowed. "She didn't call me, and I certainly would have told you if she had. Who's the judge in the case?'

Emily found a court document. "William Houston."

"I know Bill. I could ask him whether Amber approached him. He's not in here today, but I could call him."

"Would you?"

"Why don't you come out to the house? We could have some lunch, I can give Bill a call, and we can go through these notes. Maybe something will jump out at me."

She hesitated, knowing Matt would wonder where she was. But she could call him to explain.

The judge stroked his moustache. "Something's been bugging me about all this."

She sat forward. "What do you mean?"

"Something Celia was telling your mother the other day at the party."

Her stomach knotted. "You mean Celia knew something about Amber's death?"

He gave his head a quick shake. "Oh, no, I certainly don't think she had anything to do with what happened to Amber. I can't imagine that." But there was a trace of doubt in his voice.

She shuddered, remembering Celia's anger over the continued investigation. Maybe Celia had worked on getting family members on her side.

"I think it was about the lawyer. Yes, that's what it was. It was a problem with the lawyer that Celia recommended to Amber." Tilting his head, he paused. "Have you talked to her lawyer?"

"He refuses to see me."

"That's not surprising. But maybe he will talk to me."

She sat forward, kicking herself for not coming to her mother's partner earlier. "Would you?"

"I can call them both, the judge and the lawyer, right after lunch. Will you come to the house?"

"How far is it?"

"Twenty minutes at most." His vibrating phone skittered across the desk but he ignored it.

"I just have to make a quick call, let Matt know where I am." But when she tried the number, there was still no answer.

He said, "Where is he, if you don't mind my asking?"

"The police wanted to talk to him about the bombing," she said.

He grimaced. "That may take a while. We can try again when we're up at the house. He could join us."

"That would be great." Standing up, she felt strangely conflicted, knowing she would soon discover who had killed Amber and why. The answer was dangling in front of her as if on a string, almost close enough to snatch. It would soon be over.

But dread made her heart squeeze. What if the truth came too close to home, if Celia or her mother had been involved? Could she bear that?

* * *

Standing outside the police station, Matt checked his phone. Three missed calls, all from Emily. She must have found something. Calling her number, he got no answer. He left a message asking her to call. Maybe she was using the bathroom.

After a couple of minutes, he tried the number again. Still no answer. His stomach clenched. Had they found the hotel room? Found her? Heart racing, he hailed a cab, gave the hotel address, saying he would tip extra if the cabbie hurried.

The cabbie tried, but the downtown traffic was sluggish. In front of them, a bus stopped with a hiss of its air brakes. There was no room for the cabbie to pass. Pounding his fist on the seat, he watched while people got off, others got on.

Fifteen minutes later, the cab pulled up in front of the hotel. Tipping him, Matt jumped out, raced into the hotel and up the stairs. At the door to the room, he hesitated, not knowing what he would find.

She wasn't there. There was no sign of a struggle. The room looked neat, tidied up. A quick search failed to turn up a note or a cell phone, which suggested she had it with her. Had she gone for a walk? Why wasn't she answering? Hands shaking, he tried her number again. Getting no answer, he slammed his fist against the wall. Not setting up voice mail had been a huge mistake. One he wouldn't have made if he hadn't been so busy getting her into bed.

Sitting on the chair, he took some deep breaths, ran a hand through his hair.

There's an easy explanation. The ring's on mute.

No, it didn't make sense. The phone wasn't on mute. Something was wrong. Fear spiked in him, sent his heart racing. If anything happened to her, he didn't know what he would do. He jumped up, sprinted to the door. Waiting was not an option. He had to do something. He took the steps down to the lobby two at a time. At the front desk, nobody had seen her leave. She hadn't left a message. The woman at the counter found him the number for Mona's hotel. After being transferred twice, he got through to her.

"Maybe she lost the phone," Mona said after he explained why he was calling. "Or maybe she's busy. I'm sure it's nothing to worry about." Dishes clattered in the background, suggesting she was in a kitchen or dining room. "If it makes you feel any better, Harold isn't answering my calls either. It's not like him not to get back to me. Really—"

Matt cut in before she could continue. "If you hear from her, have her to call me, okay?" He asked for the number to her direct line and programmed it into his phone, although he didn't know if he could trust Mona Blackstock. She had an ex-con washing dishes in her hotel kitchen.

Back in the hotel room, he gave it a more thorough search, checking under the beds in case a note had fallen there. Nothing.

Don't panic. In a minute, she'll walk through the door with a perfectly reasonable explanation.

After ten minutes, unable to sit still, he went down to the lobby, asked again if anybody had seen her. Received the same answer. Outside, he scanned the sidewalk in front of the hotel, deserted except for three women carrying logo-imprinted paper shopping bags and, in the distance, a dozen toddlers walking two abreast with two adult chaperones.

Panic surging through him, the knot in his stomach hardened into a rock. What if those men had taken her? Should he call the police? They'd laugh at him. One of the shoppers brushed by him as she passed, and he flinched.

He tried Emily's mother again.

"Haven't heard anything." She must have left the dining room, because there was no background noise this time, just an eerie quiet. "I haven't heard from Harold, either. It's certainly not very responsible. I know he's not in court this afternoon. It's just not like him."

"Okay." He wanted to get off the phone, try Emily one last time before calling the police.

She laughed harshly. "Maybe the two of them are together."

For a moment he couldn't speak. Had Emily gone to see him? She had promised to see his new house.

He took a deep breath. "Where does Harold live?"

"I was joking." She spoke derisively.

"I'm not. Maybe she's up there, and he's giving her a tour. That's why they're not answering. Maybe they're outside."

Mona gave him the judge's address, phone number, and directions, telling him it would take about twenty minutes to get there. "Have him call me."

Hanging up, he tried Emily's phone again and then the judge's. Still no answer. But he felt a sudden light-headedness. They were together, ignoring their phones. It would explain everything.

A broken right arm was less than ideal for driving, but he didn't want to be stuck up there without a ride. He got in the car, thankful that he had rented an automatic, pulled out of the hotel parking lot, and drove through slow traffic to the main road that bisected Riverton before heading north on Highway 11 out of town, following it through the expanding suburbs as it wound through green fields toward the mountain. He checked his watch. Twenty minutes had already passed. Somewhere along here, Celia had been stopped in June on suspicion of drunk driving.

Ten miles from town, he turned right on Mountain Road, a narrow gravel track that ran alongside a lake for several miles before it reached the base of the mountain. The road dropped off abruptly to the lake, so he dropped his speed, glanced across the glistening whitecaps to the green fields on the other side.

At the end of the lake, the road began its ascent up the steep slope. Passing four houses, he drove half a mile farther to the top of the mountain until he reached the black iron gate that Mona had told him marked the entrance to the judge's property.

The gate open, he glanced at the security camera before driving down the lane and parked the car at the side of the house, a big timber frame with an attached three-car garage. He couldn't see a car, but it could be in the garage. Leaving the keys on the floor mat, he jumped out, ran up to the front door, and rang the bell.

There was no answer. Ringing it again, he noticed the camera mounted on a beam above the door. The judge wasn't joking when he said he took his security seriously. Somewhere, maybe a mile away, a chainsaw whined.

Pacing, he felt his stomach harden again. He had been wrong. And he'd just wasted half an hour. He had to call the police. The cell phone was in the car. Turning, he jumped off the porch.

The judge came to the door, rubbing his eyes. "Sorry to keep you waiting," he said. "I was just having a nap. Come in, come in. Emily said you might drop by."

"Is she here?"

"No, she was, but she left a while ago." Smiling, the judge ushered him into a large tiled foyer. "What's the matter?"

"She's not answering her cell phone." He rubbed his head. That new-house smell, off-gassing of wood and paint, filled his nostrils.

MacDonald tugged at his moustache. "She used my phone to call a cab."

"Do you know where she went?" he said, cursing Emily. What good was a cell phone if she didn't use it?"

"She went back to town, as far as I know." The judge jingled what sounded like a set of keys in his pocket.

"What cab company did she call? Can you check your phone?" He didn't remember seeing a cab on the road, but he hadn't been watching for one.

Frowning, MacDonald seemed to realize the extent of his worry. "I'll go get it. It's in the great room." He pointed to an old church pew in the foyer. "Have a seat."

He sat down, gripped by a rising nausea. He got up, walked down the wide hallway into the great room. It was massive, two stories high, with a floor-to-ceiling stone fireplace, criss-crossing beams, and a wall of windows that looked out over the mountainside to the valley below.

Hearing him, the judge turned around, his cell phone in his hand. "Let me get you a cup of coffee. Come in, sit down." He gestured to a brown leather sofa.

Matt stayed where he was. "No, thanks. Any luck?"

Putting the phone to his ear, the judge said, "I'll call them now."

Eyes darting around, Matt's eyes stopped on the wood coffee table. There were two cups on a tray. And a notebook. Amber's notebook. His throat constricted. Emily wouldn't have left that. Was she hiding from him?

Finished with the call, MacDonald slipped the phone into his pocket. "She took a cab to the Hotel Belvedere. Is that where you're staying?"

Pulse hammering, he nodded. "Are you sure she left?"

"Of course she left. Why would I say she had if she hadn't?" Eyes narrowed, the judge glared at him a moment and Matt had that feeling again that here was a man who wasn't used to being questioned. MacDonald's eyes softened, although a trace of irritation still shadowed his face.

Staring back, he felt the hairs rising on the back of his neck. "She left the notebook," he said dully, trying to think.

"She asked me to look through it."

Nodding, he turned to go. His gut told him something wasn't right. He needed to get out, to get his cell phone and call the police.

"Where are you going?"

He whirled around, something about the cold, harsh tone warning him what was coming even before he saw the gun in the judge's hand. Bile rose in his throat. "Where's Emily?" His voice rose in anger. "What have you done with her?"

"All this could have been avoided, if you'd just left it alone." Walking closer, the judge shot him a harsh look, all trace of politeness now gone. His voice hardened. "But you couldn't, could you?"

"Where is she? Tell me, you bastard."

The judge motioned with his gun toward a door at the opening of a side hallway off the foyer. "Downstairs." His cold stare suggested impatience more than anger, as if all this was just a waste of his valuable time.

Matt walked to the door, opened it, and started down the stairs. The judge followed, several steps back, giving no opportunity for Matt to do anything. The broken arm didn't help, of course.

You bastard. If she's dead, I'll kill you.

The basement was huge, dark except for a few small windows. At the far end, two rooms had been roughed in with studs. Closer to them, in a corner, a room had been built out of cement blocks. It was eighty square feet, with a steel door for an opening. To the right of the door was an open cardboard box, half filled with construction supplies.

The judge motioned him toward it. "That's my safe room. Haven't had time to have it furnished yet." His face seemed stuck in a scowl. "Never thought I'd have to use it, but here we are."

Stepping forward, the judge opened the door, and gestured for Matt to enter. The room was empty, save for one thing. Emily was cowering against the wall in a dark corner, her hands tied behind her back, duct tape over her mouth.

Confusion and shock widened her eyes before something much more potent took over. Her expression darkened and she kicked at the concrete floor with her bare feet.

She was pissed.

CHAPTER SEVENTEEN

D*amn idiot!*"

Emily mumbled the curse into the duct tape when Matt appeared in the doorway. He was the last person she'd expected to see when the door opened. It was bad enough she had been caught. But now they were both done for.

Stomping her foot on the floor, she glared at the judge. Ignoring her, he pointed to an area on one of the outside walls, which was roughed in for a toilet and sink with tubes for water lines running through the studs. "Sit down."

When Matt hesitated, the judge pointed the gun at her. "Do it or I'll shoot her."

Matt shuffled over to the wall and sat down. The judge kicked the cardboard box near the door inside the room. Reaching into it, he pulled out an open package of cable ties and a roll of duct tape, knelt down, and tied Matt's left hand to length of red tubing behind him. That done, he wrapped duct tape around Matt's mouth and checked to see if there was any-thing in his pockets.

She wanted to ask MacDonald why, but the tape over her mouth prevented her. Would it make her feel better if she knew? Probably not.

The judge stood up. "It'll be no use trying to get out. I've called in reinforcements and I can watch you from a monitor until they're here." He looked at his Rolex. "Not too long now."

At the door, he said, "Just so you know. I didn't want to do this. You forced my hand."

Her heart lurching, she searched MacDonald's face for a sign that he wouldn't deliver them to those killers. But his ex-pression was hard and implacable, betraying no battle with his conscience, in fact betraying no emotion whatsoever. A chill seized her, creeping up from her chest into her shoulders, neck, and face.

From somewhere deep in the house came a buzzing sound.

"They're early," the judge said, looking upward before he walked out, pulling the door shut behind him.

Heart pounding, she got up on her knees and crawled over to Matt. Leaning in, she moved her face close to his, ignored his surprised look, and bit at the duct tape covering his mouth. Pulling from the top down, she soon had enough tape off that he could talk.

"Let me do yours," he said.

A minute later, the tape off, she hissed, "What the hell are you doing here?"

"Nice to see you, too," he whispered with a quick roll of his eyes. "I came looking for you. Are you okay?"

"Just great. I'm actually getting quite comfortable being in enclosed spaces. The only problem is it won't matter because soon we'll both be dead." Glaring at him, she shook her head furiously. "Unbelievable."

"If you could shut up for a minute, maybe we could figure out how to get out of here. The door only locks from the inside, so it's no problem."

"Well, Einstein, it doesn't matter. You're forgetting that he's watching us on a monitor."

"I didn't see any cameras on the stairs or down here. He won't be able to see us before we get to the door."

"I'm not going up there, not alone, not with my hands tied up. See that package of cable ties over there?" She gestured with her head. "It says heavy duty in big fat letters. There's no way we can break them. And we're out of time."

"Keep your voice down," he whispered. "I have an idea. Will you try it? I can't with my broken arm."

"All right," she hissed, still angry.

"First you have to get your hands in front of you."

"What?"

"Sit down on your butt, tuck your legs to your chest, and you should be able to squeeze your hands under."

Fifteen seconds later, her hands were in front. "What now?"

"Fingernails?"

She held up her hands. "Broke those in the cave. Maybe I can work my way out." Bringing her wrists together, she tried to wriggle out but they were tied too tightly. She slammed her fists on the floor. "It's useless, and they're going to be down here any minute."

He pressed his lips together. "You'll have to break them."

"Break them? Are you nuts?" she snarled, her temper flaring again.

"Remember that course? I'll walk you through it.

"Just listen to me. Pull the ties as tight as you can. Use your teeth." She was about to say something but he gave her a warning look. "Tighter. It will make them easier to break. Keep that little locking thing in the middle, between your hands."

Ties now cutting painfully into her wrists, she looked at him.

"I've seen this done. There was a model in that course I took. She was bigger than you, and she could do it, so I know you can. I'd show you but I'm kind of tied up. You have to lift your arms above your head, way up, then bring them down quickly against your stomach. Try to bring your shoulder blades together as you do it. You have to do it quick and hard. The ties should snap at the weakest point, which is that thing in the middle."

She looked at him doubtfully, but what did she have to lose? Adrenalin pumping through her veins, she lifted her hands, squeezed her eyes shut, and slammed her fists into her stomach.

The cable tie broke. She looked up in astonishment.

"Okay, now you have to help me. Fast, before those guys upstairs finish figuring out what they're going to do and come down here."

She scrambled over. "Stop talking. Tell me what to do."

"Look in that box, find something that you can use to stick into the locking bar to lift it."

She looked in the box, found a box of finishing nails under a roll of paper towels. Kneeling beside him, she lifted up the tiny bar. The tie slid out.

They opened the door, then crept across the floor to the bottom of the stairs. The door at the top was closed. As they climbed the stairs, they could hear voices. People talking, perhaps in the kitchen, rising above classical piano music playing in the background. She strained to hear. Two people. One was the judge. The other voice was a woman's.

A pain gripped her stomach, as if she'd been punched. "That's my mother," she whispered.

Matt, who had stopped on a stair above, reached down and squeezed her hand. "It doesn't mean she has anything to do with this. But I don't think those guys are here yet. We have to try to get out. If your mother's in on it—and I'm not saying she is—she's not going to help us."

"If she isn't, I don't want to put her in danger."

"We'll call police as soon as we're outside. There's a cell phone in my car."

The sharp click of heels on a tiled floor signaled that Mona, at least, was in the kitchen.

Matt looked at her. "Ready?"

She nodded. "If you go right, there's a side door just down the hallway to the garage. That's the way I came in."

Opening the door, he slipped out, took her hand. As they crept down the hallway, the sound of water running and the banging of pots and pans emerged from the kitchen.

"That's odd, Harold." It was Mona's voice.

"What?"

"The security panel says your basement door opened."

Emily froze, her heart hammering. Matt tugged her toward the door, reached for the knob.

"Stop right there." The judge's voice boomed down the hallway.

She turned around. MacDonald's large frame filled the opening of the hallway. In his hand was a gun.

Mona approached from behind, looked at them quizzically. "What's going on?" Coming closer, she looked at the gun in Harold's hand, perplexed. Her mouth falling open, she shuffled back a couple of steps.

"What do you think?" He gestured with the gun to Mona. "Get over there with them."

"What?" Ashen faced, she held her arms limply at her sides, not moving.

"Move!"

He yelled it this time, and Mona walked to Emily's side and clutched her daughter's arm. "What is this all about?" She looked from Emily to Matt, as if one of them held the explanation.

MacDonald gestured angrily toward Emily with the gun. "What it's all about, my dear, is your nosy daughter," he snapped. "She's ruined it for you."

Mona glanced at her a moment, then back at the judge. "We're going to get married. You promised me." Lips pressed into a thin line, she pitched her voice high. "At least tell me why."

"I had a nice little arrangement at the courthouse. It helped build this house, which God knows I deserved after all those years. Amber found out and was threatening to go to the police."

"You killed Amber?" Scowling, Mona narrowed her eyes. "If you needed money, why didn't you just ask? I would have given it to you."

Mona clenched her fists. Red splotches colored her cheeks and spittle gathered at the corners of her mouth. Shock appeared to be giving way to anger as her eyes drilled holes into the judge.

Outside the house, a car screeched to a halt near the front door. "My backup's here." The judge glanced at the front door.

A look of rage filling her face, Mona charged at him. In the next instant, Matt swung his cast at the judge. The gun discharged, fell, and skidded across the floor.

Matt jumped on top of the judge, pinned him to the floor. Scooping up the gun, she ran to her mother. There was blood coming from a wound in her right arm. Mona stared at it, not comprehending, her face blotchy with anger.

There was banging at the front door.

Matt looked up, his black-brown eyes flashing with fierce determination. "Get your mom to the safe room. Lock the door. Try to stop the bleeding."

"What about you?"

"I'll be okay."

"I can't leave you alone up here."

"I'm going to drive away, get out." He looked at her, his eyes scanning her face, as if he were memorizing it. "Can you trust me?"

She nodded.

"Then trust me when I say I'll be okay. You'll be safe downstairs. I'll call for help."

She hesitated a moment before handing him the gun.

"Go!"

Putting her arm around her mother, they hurried down to the safe room, locked the door behind them. She helped her mother sit down. She tore off a square of paper towel from the roll in the box and placed it over the wound, lifted it, and took a closer look. It was a thin graze, about two inches long, with jagged tears along the outside. It didn't look deep, although it was still bleeding. Covering the paper towel with a rag, she grabbed the duct tape, tore off a strip, and wrapped it around her mother's arm several times.

Standing up, she put her ear to the door, listened for a minute. Nothing. What if Matt was up there, dead?

Her mother was sweating and trembling, taking rapid, shallow gasps for air.

"It's okay, Mother." She sat down and put her arm around her. "The bullet scraped you. It didn't go in. You're going to be okay."

Ashen faced, Mona seemed not to hear. She squeezed her eyes shut, pressed her fists to the side of her head. "My chest hurts. I can't breathe."

"Take a deep breath." Emily tried to sooth her. Was she having a heart attack? Given what just happened, it wouldn't surprise her. "Just hang on, help is coming."

It was maybe ten minutes later, although it seemed forever, before she heard the first sirens and knew help was on the way. A few minutes after that, out of the house, Mona was loaded on a stretcher. There were half a dozen emergency vehicles in the driveway—police cars, ambulances, and a fire truck, all with lights flashing—and a dozen people in uniform. Emily scoured the faces. There was no sign of Matt, or the judge.

* * *

Matt knew what he had to do. Divert attention from Emily and Mona. That meant leading the judge's henchmen away from the house. And he had to take the judge with him.

"Give me your cell phone," he said to the judge. "And your keys. I know they're in your pocket."

Handing them over, the judge growled. "You won't get out of here."

"We'll see about that."

At least one of the men was banging on the front door, shouting to get in.

Matt glanced around the corner of the side hallway into the great room. At the back of the house, leading to the deck, were three sets of patio doors. He couldn't see anybody, but didn't think it would be too difficult for them to find a place to break in.

He would have to escape through the garage. "Let's go." Putting the gun on the judge's back, he shoved him down the hallway to the door leading to the garage. A screen mounted on the wall near the door showed video from six different outside locations. Two men were circling around to the back of the house. He'd stick with the plan to take the judge's car. His car might be blocked in.

In the garage, he grabbed a roll of duct tape off a pegboard on the wall, tied the judge's hands behind his back, and opened the rear door of the compact silver sedan. "Get in and get down, because they might start shooting."

Putting the gun in his back waistband, he climbed in the front seat, buckled his seat belt, and pushed the button to start the car. He pulled down the visor and pushed the garage door opener. Grinding noisily, it started slowly upward.

Tensing, Matt waited just long enough to ensure they were clear of the door and then gunned the car out of the garage. As it shot up the driveway, he caught a glimpse of a long black sedan blocking in his car. It had tinted windows and the size and shape of a police car. The rearview mirror showed a man running from the side of the garage toward the driveway.

Big Guy.

At the top of the driveway, he stopped, dialed 911, spent ten seconds explaining the emergency. "There are two women in a safe room in the basement. One has a gunshot wound." He threw the phone onto the seat beside him.

Two men jumped into the black sedan. Sure now that they were coming, he turned onto the gravel road. Gripping the wheel with his left hand, he pressed his foot down hard on the gas. He shot down the road, the car trailing a cloud of dust like gray smoke.

After a minute, the road began its steep descent down the mountain to the lake. The black sedan closed the gap between them. Big Guy was driving, leaning forward, both hands on the wheel. The sedan got even closer, until the chrome grille filled his rearview mirror.

Fishtailing on the gravel, Matt's tires spraying dust and gravel as they fought for purchase, he struggled to keep compact car in the middle of the road. The judge unleashed an expletive-laced rant about how they were going to crash. Ignoring him, he stepped on the gas pedal. The smell of burning rubble filled his lungs.

Gaining speed, the sedan moved to his left, trying pull up alongside. He swerved left, tried to cut it off. Scowling, Big Guy bumped his rear corner and the compact lurched forward.

The passenger in the pursuing car leaned out the window and fired off a burst of shots that hit metal with four quick pops.

Ducking, he felt the car slide to the right as the road began to level off. Ahead was the lake. He straightened the car out, ducked again as the sedan gained. The judge wasn't shouting anymore, but blubbering. It meant he was still alive. He wanted the bastard alive.

Where were the cops?

Just ahead, the blue-green water of the lake loomed on the left side of the road, down a steep embankment.

He was out of options. The sedan's front tires were now in line with the back of his car. All Big Guy had to do now was slam into him and he would spin off the road.

In the next instant the rear side window exploded, spraying a torrent of glass through the car, pelting his neck. Something kicked his arm, maybe a big chunk of gravel. Glancing at it, he saw a splotch of red. Pulse hammering in his throat, he cursed. He had been shot. In his good arm.

Time to try something new.

Easing of the pedal slightly, he waited until the sedan's front tires were in line with the center of his car. Angling left, he smashed his car into the sedan. He slammed on the brakes and pulled the wheel to the right. The cars smashed with a loud crunch of metal.

The sedan spun out off the road and flew over the embankment into the lake.

Slamming on the brakes, he glanced in the backseat. The judge was breathing, didn't look like he'd been shot. As Matt stepped out of the car, the tail end of the sedan disappeared underwater, like a sinking ship. He waited, holding his breath. A rescue attempt was not a way to cap the afternoon, not with a cast on one arm and bullet hole in the other.

Twenty seconds after that, one man surfaced. Big Guy soon followed, his head bobbing in the water like a buoy.

CHAPTER EIGHTEEN

At the hospital, Mona Blackstock was whisked off to the emergency room, the doctors more concerned about a possible heart attack than her gunshot wound.

Emily paced in the hallway, unable to get her mind off Matt. Dark images played in her mind. Of him being captured. Killed. *Trust me*, he'd said. *I'll be all right.*

How stupid of her. Of course he wasn't all right. A sick dread convulsed her stomach.

An hour later, the gunshot wound bandaged up, her mother was transferred to a private room on the fourth floor. The doctor wanted to keep her overnight to run tests.

"Any news?" her mother said.

Shaking her head, Emily pulled up a chair. Her mother looked frail and tired, not the strong woman she was used to seeing. A police officer had talked to them both, but said more formal interviews could wait until the next day.

"I'm sure Matt will be all right," her mother said.

Emily rubbed her face, marveling at how easily her mother tossed that out. She wasn't sure of that at all.

"As for Harold, he can go straight to hell." Her mother spit saliva as she spoke. "I wasted too many years on him. No wonder he kept saying he wanted this mess cleared up before we got married. He kept pestering me to see the chief."

Emily felt her mouth drop. "What? Is that why you wanted the investigation stopped?" Her pulse speeding, she rounded on her mother. "Why didn't you tell me?"

Chastised, her mother lowered her eyes. "You wanted me to be happy, didn't you?"

"Not at the expense of finding out what happened to Amber." Emily ground her teeth. "I can't believe you went along with him."

A whimper escaped her mother's lips. "How was I supposed to know he was responsible for Amber being dead? Besides, I had my sister to think of. Someone had to protect Jean. She almost had a nervous breakdown after the investigation was reopened."

Emily bit back the retort on the tip of her tongue. It was no use arguing when her mother had found a way to justify her behavior. Instead, she said, "I'm just glad you didn't get married."

"I was nowhere near ready to marry him." Her mother snorted, recovering now. "I told him he had to get clear of his money problems before that would happen."

Remembering that her mother had blamed her for the delay, Emily gritted her teeth and decided not to pursue the point. What was the use? She said, "Money problems?"

"He was never good with money. He spent way too much on that house. How did he ever expect to pay for it?"

A few minutes later, as her mother drifted off to sleep, the news came on the small television above her bed. The video showed police cruisers in front of the house. She recognized the tall, lanky frame of the police chief, Frank Cameron, beside the cruiser. A man beside him looked like Sam Fisher, although she couldn't be sure. A line of police tape across the top of the driveway kept news crews back. The reporter didn't seem to know too much and made no mention of Matt or the judge.

Her stomach rolled over as a sick dread gripped her. As more time passed, she had to face up to the fact that Matt was likely dead. Instead of worrying about her mother, she should have been with him. At the very least, she should have told him she loved him. Because she did. But now it was too late. She wanted to scream. Clutching her stomach, she slumped back in the chair.

A few minutes later, the doctor popped her head in the door and motioned for her to join her in the hallway. A matronly woman with dark tortoiseshell glasses, she had a manila file folder in her hand. "Your mother's electrocardiogram is normal. I'd still like to keep her overnight, but she's going to be fine."

She raised her eyebrows. "So she didn't have a heart attack? What was it?"

The doctor toyed with a candy-pink stethoscope around her neck. "I'm pretty sure it was an anxiety attack."

Emily uttered a soft curse. A panic attack? That was way better than a heart attack. She gave her head a little shake. The attack had started in the safe room. Her mother had claustrophobia. It all made sense. Her mother never took the elevator at work, saying she preferred the stairs. Emily had bought it. How many other signs had she missed?

Her mother was still sleeping, so she walked down the hallway and sat in an empty waiting room to wait for the news to come on at the top of the hour. When it did, she turned the volume up, stared at the screen as the announcer said one man had been shot. Three people were being questioned. One was a judge, unnamed.

Panic gripped her, twisting her insides. Had Matt been shot? How bad was it? In the hallway, she approached a young nurse who promised to ask if anybody had been admitted with a gunshot wound. She clutched her seesawing stomach as she watched the nurse step behind a desk, pick up a phone. When she finished with the call, she motioned Emily over. A man with a gunshot wound was on a surgical unit two floors below. She didn't know his name or condition.

Thanking her, Emily raced down the stairs, emerged two flights down onto a busier floor. Machines beeped in patients' room. A nurse rushed by her in the hallway and disappeared into a patient's room. At the nurses' station, a uniformed cop was leaning over the counter, talking to a woman in scrubs with purple hair sitting behind a computer.

Heart pounding, she approached them, explained who she was. The cop told her a man named Matt Herrington had been admitted with a gunshot wound. He started giving her an update, telling her three men were in custody, including a Harold MacDonald.

Cutting him short, she asked the nurse for Matt's room number. Right now, she didn't care about anything but that he was all right.

A minute later, she stood in the open doorway of Matt's room. It was in semidarkness and he appeared to be sleeping, hooked up to an intravenous line and a few different machines that displayed results on a glowing screen beside the bed. Choking back a sob, she crept in, not wanting to wake him.

"Hello there."

"You're awake." She rushed to his side.

"I don't know how the hell you're supposed to get any sleep in these places. It's so bloody noisy. Between the nurses and the police, I'm going crazy."

"Do you want me to go?"

"Hell, no, but see if you can lock the door to keep everyone else out."

She smiled. "How are you?"

"I'm fine. Took a bullet to the arm, had to have the cast reset on the other arm, but I'm okay. Groggy as hell. Can't think straight. Keep falling asleep."

She wiped away a tear. "Cranky, too."

He rolled his eyes. "Yeah, well, you don't have a monopoly on crankiness." He reached for her with his right arm. "Come closer."

Sitting on the bed, she clenched her mouth, trying to hold

back tears. She didn't want to ever let him out of her sight again. His half-closed eyes were fighting a losing battle with sleep.

"Go to sleep," she said.

His eyes drifted open. "How's your mother?"

"She's fine." Taking hold of his hand, she stroked the rough texture. "Did you hear anything about your father?"

"He's okay. It's some sort of hernia, but he doesn't have to have surgery, at least not now."

When she asked him what happened after he left the judge's house, he described being chased and shot until the other car went off the road into a lake. Police arriving on the scene suspected he had kidnapped MacDonald and they escorted him to hospital, where doctors decided removing the bullet could do more harm than leaving the slug in his arm. That was when the real fun had begun, hours of interrogation before police began to see things his way.

She smiled. "You'll be happy to know MacDonald is in custody. The police will conduct an investigation—"

He closed his eyes. "I don't care about that shit."

She drew her hand away. "What do you mean?"

"We've wasted too much time. I've been trying to keep awake, waiting for you to come. I need your help."

"My help?"

"I'm trying to figure out if I want a relationship with a friend of mine."

Her heart lurched. "What kind of friend?" Her lips had trouble forming the words.

"A cranky one. Useless at …relationships." His voice was fading.

Attempting to process what he was saying, she looked away. Clear liquid dripped steadily from an intravenous tube into his arm. On the computer next to his bed, thin digital lines formed jagged peaks as they moved across the screen. If they hooked her up, they would be spiking erratically. They'd have to call a code blue.

"Well?"

Swallowing, she looked at him again. "She sounds like my kind of person. But this is a bit sudden. And I'm not sure you should be talking about this in your frame of mind."

"There's nothing wrong with my frame of mind." Reaching for her hand, those black-brown eyes stared into hers for a moment, then fluttered closed.

* * *

When Matt woke early the next morning, Emily was sleeping in a chair pulled up close beside the bed. A blanket tucked under her chin, her dark hair fell gently against her pale, translucent face. His eyes drank in every feature, the delicate line of her nose, the full lips. Light roots were starting to show in her dark hair. He longed to see the natural color.

Some sixth sense must have told her she was watching him, because her eyes opened.

He said, "Did you have a good sleep?"

She gave a little shake of her head, sat up straight, rubbed her eyes. "Awful, if you want to know the truth. I had a dream we were in a cave. You were forcing me to go down. You said if I didn't you'd kill me."

He smiled. "What happened?"

"I told you to stuff it. That's where the dream ended."

"I can see some things haven't changed. I was just thinking of when I first saw you, when I pulled you out of the water. You looked like a nymph of the sea, so beautiful. It didn't take long to find out how cranky nymphs could be."

She smirked. "You were pretty cranky yourself last night."

"Was I? Yesterday was a blur."

Sometime during the night she must have washed up, because she smelled of soap and was wearing a hospital scrub top, white with navy-blue trim, that looked miles too big.

He said, "How's your mom today?"

"She's fine. For a while, we thought she might have had a heart attack, but she didn't, thankfully." She told him about the doctor's suspicions of a panic attack. "I'd never seen her have one before, but she must have."

He gave her a puzzled look. "Yet she gave you such a hard time about being claustrophobic."

"I don't want to even try to figure out the psychology of that one," she said slowly. "But it's funny, because I was okay in the safe room. Maybe because I was so busy, first getting us untied, then looking after my mother."

The door to his room opened and the police chief, Frank Cameron, came in, pushing Mona in a wheelchair. As Emily stood, the chief pushed the wheelchair to the far side of the bed. He told Emily he preferred to stand and she should sit down.

After a few minutes of pleasantries, the chief said, "I thought I would give you all an update here."

Matt said, "What's the judge's story now? Is he still claiming to be the victim of a home invasion?"

Mona snorted. "That's ridiculous. He's going to get away with it, isn't he?"

The chief shook his head. "Not a chance. As Matt pointed out to us yesterday, he ended up doing himself in."

Emily looked at him, eyebrows raised.

The chief said, "We know that he wasn't kidnapped or the victim of a home invasion—and that he, in fact, shot Mona—because we spent the better part of the night looking at security footage from inside the home."

Emily let out a long sigh. "Of course, thank God for that. And thank God for the safe room, although I didn't think so the first time he put me in there." She swallowed, looked up with steady eyes. "Who killed Amber and why?"

Cameron said, "Amber was killed by hit men, on orders from Harold MacDonald."

"Why?" Emily seemed composed, ready to accept the news.

"We got some information from MacDonald late last night, after we showed him some of the incriminating video. Amber found out about a corruption scheme operating out of the courthouse. She got suspicious when her lawyer, Joel Ackerman, kept pushing for a higher settlement. We think MacDonald was pushing the judge in her case to approve it. The plan was for MacDonald and Ackerman to pocket some of that money, about fifty thousand dollars. That's above the fees the lawyer would get."

The next question came from Mona. "Is Ackerman admitting this?"

"Not yet, but he's in custody and the feds have taken over the investigation. They'll get to the bottom of it. It sounds like there's at least one other lawyer involved."

Emily said, "How did Amber find out?"

"Celia Williams suggested Amber use Ackerman as her lawyer. Celia had a DUI charge that Ackerman and MacDonald got rid of. Amber found out about that."

Mona snorted. "I knew something was going on with Celia. She was acting so strange."

Matt exchanged a look with Emily, who gave a quick roll of her eyes.

He said, "What will happen with that charge?"

"That's up to the prosecutor, but the case will have to be looked at again. We don't know yet how much she paid them, if at all. But to get back to Amber, it sounds like she had suspicions about her insurance case, and then when she found out about Celia's DUI it all started to fall into place. She refused to go along with it, even though she would have gotten more money in the settlement."

Emily said, "So who exactly killed her?"

"MacDonald had a couple of guys working for him. One of them is his son-in-law." He turned to Mona. "His name is Philip March. He's an ex-cop. Do you know him?"

She said, "I met him once, a couple of years ago when they came for a visit. He's a big guy, bigger even than Harold. He and his wife, Sylvia, Harold's daughter, live in Chicago."

The chief said, "He'll soon be living in a prison cell and I'd be surprised if he ever got out."

Emily and Matt exchanged another look. Big Guy. It would be nice to see him behind bars.

Mona looked at the chief. "What will happen to Harold?"

The chief looked at her closely. "If he's convicted, he'll go to jail. Right now, he's cooperating to beat a conspiracy to murder charge, but the corruption alone is enough to put him away for a very long time. It will take a long time for the feds to get to the bottom of all this. They'll have to reopen a lot of old cases. A lot of them are small. He'd take a couple of hundred bucks to change somebody's probation terms so they could report monthly rather than weekly."

Matt said, "How did they find out where Emily was hiding?"

The chief looked at Emily. "Apparently, you did a search on your mother's computer. MacDonald looked at the search history, found a link to the resort, and put two and two together."

Emily nodded. "Of course. That was stupid of me."

Matt said, "Don't beat yourself up about that. You had no way of knowing." He turned to the chief. "Do you know who attacked Emily?"

She said, "I know it wasn't this Philip March. He's too big. And three men found me at the cabin."

The chief said, "The feds will sort that out. They won't get away with it." He looked at Mona. "Shall I wheel you back?"

She nodded, looked at her daughter. "I'll likely be discharged this morning. The doctor says I'm well enough to go home."

Emily got to her feet. "I'll make sure you get home."

Mona stopped her with a gesture. "That's okay. Frank has that covered." She smiled warmly at the chief.

Emily walked over and kissed her mother on the cheek and they thanked the police chief.

The door shut, he said, "I think there may be something going on between the two of them."

"I think you're right. I just hope he doesn't move in with her." At his puzzled look, she said, "Celia wouldn't be able to sell him that house."

He smiled. "That will be the least of her worries. I have a feeling she'll be under a lot of scrutiny." He made a mental note to follow up on the pictures he'd taken of the hit men chasing Emily, see if there was anything the police could use.

"I'm just wondering how much the chief let my mother cloud his judgment about Amber's murder investigation. And I feel bad, too, because maybe Amber suspected the judge but didn't want to say anything because of my mother's relationship with him."

His breakfast came. She watched for a second while he tried to eat, then grabbed the spoon out of his hands to feed him herself.

He was swallowing a mouthful of runny egg when his cell phone rang. It was on the night table. She picked it up, handed it to him in his left hand. He put it on speakerphone. It was a call from his work in Boston.

Emily slipped out of the room, returned five minutes after he'd finished the call, and sat down on the bed. "Is everything all right?"

"The construction supervisor and one of the foremen are having a disagreement over excavation at a fourplex we're just starting. It's nothing that can't be sorted out, but I do have to get back. There's a lot of really expensive equipment sitting idle. I'm going to see about a flight out tomorrow."

Something dark flickered in her eyes and they began to shimmer. "So I guess you've forgotten what you said last night?"

"I was pretty groggy. What did I say?"

"Nothing important." Standing up, she walked to the window and looked out, wiping her eyes with the back of her hand.

He said, "What will you do?"

When she turned around, she'd lifted her chin and composure masked her face. "I have to think about that, but I do know I want to get out of Riverton."

He said, "You need a plan."

That mask slipped a little, revealing a glint of anger. "Right. Well, I guess I should get going, get working on that."

He smiled at her. "You're getting ornery again."

"Ornery? That's a new word." Her tone was clipped.

"Lucky for you that I have a thing for ornery people."

She arched an eyebrow.

"Some of my memory is coming back from last night. I seem to remember you saying you would consider a move to Boston."

She pushed away from the wall, a small smile flitting on her lips. "I don't quite remember agreeing to that."

"Well, how about it? I hear Boston has a couple of good law schools."

Her eyes narrowed. "I thought you'd forgotten—"

"You think I would forget about that? Not a chance."

She came toward him, sat on the bed, and maneuvered her way into his arms. "I love you, Matt Herrington. Not from first sight—it's more like you've grown on me."

"Do me a favor?" He looked into those eyes, bright and soulful, and knew he would never tire of them. He would never tire of her.

"What?" She drew her face close enough to see the faint freckles on her nose.

He kissed her, slowly, deeply, moved his lips down over her jaw to that soft, creamy neck before stopping to nibble on an ear. "Go lock that door," he whispered.

Please see the next page for a preview of the next book in Alex Kingwell's Chasing Justice series!

CHAPTER ONE

Nicky Bosko didn't see the beat cop until it was too late. She was thirty steps from the intersection, and he was tucked in around the corner, his eyes tracking a homeless man pushing a shopping cart in front of her down the rain-slicked sidewalk.

Her heart constricted, as if someone had reached in and grabbed it. The girl walking beside Nicky followed her gaze, froze.

Nicky grabbed the girl's arm. "Keep walking." She pitched her voice low.

They had no choice. A cold drizzle had emptied the sidewalks, and the cop would notice them for sure if they turned back or tried to cross the street. They had to keep going and pass by him.

The girl had that deer-in-the-headlights look, her eyes as wide as saucers. "He'll see me." The words seemed to catch in her throat.

"No, he won't." Nicky tried to sound confident even as her stomach twisted into a hard knot.

The cop, his hands hooked behind his back, was ruddy-faced, stout, and wore a dark rain jacket. He stood under an awning, partially protected from the rain, which a west wind drove down at a slant toward him.

The homeless guy stopped to peer into a mesh garbage can, parking his cart at an angle that blocked the sidewalk.

Stuck behind him, the knot in Nicky's gut tightened. Forcing herself not to look at the cop, she focused on the homeless guy. Fat raindrops slid down the green garbage bag he wore as a poncho.

The girl's eyes darted around, as if looking for an escape route. Nicky tightened her grip on her arm as the homeless man finished inspecting the garbage can. Straightening, he wheeled the cart to the left, having decided to take the cross street. He waited at the curb for a green pedestrian signal.

Nicky and the girl kept going straight ahead. Just as they reached the curb, the pedestrian light flashed yellow. They could cross with the homeless man, who was now in the intersection, but it seemed better not to backtrack. Not to do anything that might draw the attention of the cop.

She bit the inside of her cheek, cursed under her breath. Cars and buses cruised by, their tires hissing on the wet road and spitting up water. Wiping rain from her forehead, she glanced to the right, past the cop and up the side street. Dark clouds hung low in the bleak sky. On the other side of the drugstore was an office building, then a four-story parking lot. On the next block, a patrol car pulled to the side of the road.

She held her breath until two officers got out and walked into a building.

There were two ways this could go. They could run now in any direction. The cop would call for help, give chase and chances were one or both of them would be caught, possibly before they got farther than a block or two. Or they could keep walking. Hope the cop didn't recognize the girl. She wore Nicky's navy rain jacket and a ball cap pulled down low over her forehead, but her picture was everywhere and, since her father was a cop, there'd be extra incentive to catch this runaway. A vivid memory surfaced, something she hadn't thought about in years. She'd been fourteen, a terrified runaway huddled on a city sidewalk, begging for change. A cop had taken her to a shelter. That wouldn't happen with Michelle. This cop, any cop, would deliver her back to her father.

If this cop recognized her, then they'd run.

She shot another glance at the girl. Her name was Michelle Stafford and she was five foot six, almost Nicky's height, thirteen years old. Her soft, tiny facial features were still that of a child, but a somber guardedness in those gray-blue eyes suggested she'd already witnessed too much of life's dark side. That and the large bruise yellowing on her left cheek.

Nicky tightened her fists as a sudden fierce resolve coursed through her. She felt like a mama bear protecting her cub. The cops wouldn't get Michelle, not if she could help it.

Four people now waited with them to cross the street. She snuck a glance back at the cop. He caught her eye, gave her the onceover. Looking away, she sucked in a ragged breath, and caught a whiff of wet cement that reminded her of running track in high school. Practicing sprints and hurdles in the chill fall air. She'd been fast, probably still was. The girl would be, too.

The cop didn't look fast. But maybe he wouldn't need to be.

Holding her breath, waiting for him to shout at them to stop, she kept him in her peripheral vision. Ready to run if he moved a single step.

A car honked its horn. She jumped, swallowed hard. Beside her, a woman in hospital scrubs spoke loudly into a cell phone. Somebody had botched the grooming of her dog. Coco now had an eye infection and the woman wanted everybody in Riverton in on that little tidbit. Across the street, a woman in red running shorts bounced up and down on her toes, impatient to cross.

The girl didn't say anything, just stood, her body rigid, staring straight ahead.

At last the light changed. Starting across the intersection, Nicky kept a steadying hand on the girl's arm and forced herself not to hurry, to go with the flow. Not until they were on the other side of the street did she let out a heavy breath.

A tear escaped Michelle's eye and flowed down the middle of her bruised cheek. Nicky squeezed her hand. "Just a couple more blocks, Michelle. You'll be okay."

She scanned the sidewalk. A young guy in a jean jacket and baggy pants stared at her as he walked toward them. He wasn't looking at Michelle, but Nicky kept her eye on him until they passed. Paranoia strikes deep.

Michelle had arrived at the shelter last week, brought in by another kid after two nights on the streets. This morning, they'd convinced her to see a doctor. Nicky thought about what the doctor had told her, while Michelle was using the bathroom. Her throat soured. No wonder she'd run away. But that was a whole other worry.

A block from the shelter, the sun broke through the low clouds, and flashed off car windshields. More people spilled onto the sidewalks. That was good and bad. She and Michelle weren't as exposed, but it'd be harder to tell if they were being followed. Not that she had any skills on that front. She was a youth worker, not some covert operator.

Her eyes swept the length of the street, taking in the four people in a bus shelter up ahead. And just past them a woman in a tight cobalt-blue dress was leaning against a door, smoking a cigarette. Across the road, a man walking a muscular dog stopped to read a menu posted outside a new pizzeria. Cars streamed by. Nobody slowed or seem to take any interest in them.

Rolling her shoulders, she tried to shake off some of the tension. She felt sweaty despite the September chill and her damp hair and clothes.

The cigarette smoker ground the butt into the sidewalk, smoothed her dress then vanished inside a shoe shop.

Nicky pointed out a department store just past the shoe shop. "They have a section for teens upstairs. We could go check it out if you'd like."

The girl brightened. "Oh, please. I hardly have any clothes." Her voice was soft, surprisingly low-pitched. "One of the girls lent me a T-shirt and a pair of jeans, but they're too big."

Nicky smiled. Those were the most words the girl had

strung together in two days. It'd been hard to tell if she was naturally quiet or had switched off because of everything she'd been through.

Two minutes later, they turned the final corner before the youth shelter. The tan brick building was on the other side of the street, down half a block. Out front, in a no-parking zone, a man leaned against a dark gray sedan. Tall and broad-shouldered, he wore a light shirt and dark pants.

Nicky stopped short. Something needled at the edge of her brain. It took a second more to process what it was. The kids were all inside, not hanging out in the sunshine on the front steps.

The man was a cop.

Her heart pounding against her ribs, she reached into her shoulder bag, fished out her cell phone and shoved it into Michelle's hand.

The cop looked in their direction. Seeing them, he uncrossed his arms, pushed himself away from the car, then pulled out his wallet and flashed a badge.

She said, "Call the shelter tonight. The number's programmed in there." Her eyes searched the girl's face. "Promise?"

Michelle glanced at the man, then back at Nicky. She nodded as she clasped the cell phone. She was already up on the balls of her feet, just waiting for the go-ahead.

Nicky said, "Remember that department store? Go in there. There's an exit at the back to the next street over." She pressed some bills from her wallet into the girl's hand. "Hide out for a couple of hours, then phone. Don't use your own phone. Promise?"

Michelle's lips trembled and her eyes flicked between Nicky and the cop. "Promise."

The cop stood by his car watching them, swinging his arms.

Michelle turned, bolted up the street. She slowed for a second to hook the knapsack on both shoulders but didn't look back. She was fast, all right. Her long legs flew over the pavement.

Nicky turned back to the cop. He was halfway across the street, a hand outstretched to stop cars. His mouth was open in surprise, his eyes locked onto her.

A glance up the street showed her Michelle had disappeared. Nicky felt a sudden lightness. Michelle was the main thing. If she got away it'd be a bonus.

Nicky set off in the opposite direction Michelle had taken. Holding the shoulder bag with one hand against her chest, she raced to the next corner, catching a glimpse of the cop sprinting up the sidewalk before she rounded the corner of a smaller side street. She bolted down the street, nearly tripping, weaving in and around people, not bothering to look back now. A woman pushing a stroller swore at her.

Up ahead was a park. Darting through open wrought-iron gates, she ran down a set of concrete steps, jumped the railing near the bottom and landed heavily on her feet on a patch of grass. She crouched down next to the concrete, and tried to catch her breath.

The park took up a small city block. Just ahead in the center was a large ornate fountain, surrounded by manicured flower beds set in a sweep of lawn. Small trees lined the perimeter. It was a place people came to sit for a few minutes. Nobody in their right mind would come to hide. It was too open, exposed.

Two young men in suits sitting on a bench gave her a look. A hard stare convinced them to lose interest. The steady rush of water splashing in the fountain all but drowned out sounds from the street above. To her right, at one end of the park, another set of stairs led to a small church. It was white clapboard, one of the oldest in the state, its doors open to tourists. And fugitives. Time to move again.

Half crouching, she peered over her shoulder up the stairs. No sign of the cop. Taking a deep breath, her bag secured across her chest, she stood up, turned around.

And slammed into something hard as a wall. She bit her lip and tasted blood. Blinking, she tried to pull back but was spun around, both arms yanked behind her back.

The cop.

"Take it easy, will you?" she shouted as the handcuffs snapped shut.

CHAPTER TWO

When the cop whirled Nicky back around, she found herself staring at a broad, muscled chest. No wonder her nose felt like it'd been smashed into a wall. He had plenty through the arms and shoulders, too, and stood at least a head taller than her.

The word "strapping" came to mind. It would be perfectly natural for him to start thumping his chest and yelling a Tarzan-like call of the jungle. How he had managed to move so quickly was a marvel.

Shifting back a half step, her glance moved up his chest—lingering momentarily on the man cleavage peeking out from two undone buttons—to his face.

The curse emerged out loud this time. His eyes were intense. Not just the color, a clear, medium blue, but the way they seemed to examine every inch of her face. But not in a way that suggested he liked what he saw. If anything, it was the opposite. Like the way a rude plastic surgeon might react when presented with a particularly nasty facial disfigurement.

Swallowing hard, she took a full step back. Something weird was going on.

Those eyes not leaving her, he let go of her arm, took out his wallet and stuck a shiny metal badge in her face. Police investigator, it said. He brushed sweat from his brow with his forearm, then pocketed the badge.

"What the hell did you run for? Don't tell me you didn't see the badge." Still catching his breath, he relaxed his scrutiny of her and leaned over, putting his hands on his knees.

The question seemed rhetorical and she wasn't about to answer anyway. Not asking about Michelle didn't make sense, but maybe he wasn't too smart. Not that he looked dull, but you couldn't judge a book by its cover.

Not getting an answer, he curled his lip in disgust, reached down for her handbag and rummaged through it. Finding nothing of interest, he put it under his arm, then used his cell phone to request a car to pick them up and for someone to fetch the sedan parked outside the shelter.

Off the phone, he looked at her again. He'd caught his breath, and seemed less angry, but his odd expression suggested he remained convinced she was an alien life form.

An alien life form he was not. He was an excellent example of the male human species, in fact. Impressive eyebrows, a strong jaw, and a long, straight nose on a squarish face still flushed from exertion. The dark blond hair was messy and in need of a trim, but it combined with the stubble on his chin to give an impression of rough, raw masculinity more in keeping with thugs than cops. He'd be a natural at undercover work.

Finished with the call, he put the phone on his belt, took hold of her arm again.

The manhandling she could do without, but she had to keep her cool. She had to cut herself some slack for running, but antagonizing him further would be a fool's errand. And he'd stopped looking at her as if she were some kind of freak, the scowl on his face now reflecting that mix of irritation, suspicion, and disgust cops wore so well.

A small crowd had gathered. A chubby girl licking an ice-cream cone resisted the efforts of her father to tug her away. Behind the girl, a teenaged boy videotaped the incident. The suits had returned to their nine-to-five jobs.

She rolled her eyes at the teenager. Didn't he have anything better to do?

The cop said, "Let's go." Holding her arm, he put his hand on her upper arm and led her up the stairs. At the top, avoiding the stares of passersby, she snuck another look at the cop. His blue shirt brought out the color in those penetrating eyes. He would wear blue a lot; she'd bet good money that he was the vain type. The shirt had a logo on it, a little pony. Why did people do that, make themselves walking advertisements for clothing companies?

A few minutes later, a squad car pulled up. He helped her inside. The cop talked with the driver, but the radio chatter was too loud for her to make it out. She tried to come up with a game plan, but quickly abandoned the effort in favor of just winging it. She crossed her fingers that Michelle would be able to hide out for a couple of hours until the cops released her.

Inside the station, she drew a few looks as they walked off

the elevator through the squad room. On a far wall, behind some cubicles, a bulletin board displayed pictures of missing people. Michelle was front and center, smiling in a school photo. Nicky averted her gaze as the cop led her down a hallway to a small office, where he gestured toward a chair. He dumped her bag on the floor beside her, then left without saying anything or looking at her.

Somebody was clearly still pissed.

The office was small, too small for the two desks, three chairs, a bookcase, and a tall metal cabinet that had been crammed into it. On the ceiling were those large white Styrofoam tiles, held in place by steel brackets. Some were crooked, exposing long strands of red and black wires.

A minute later, the cop returned and asked her to stand, then removed the handcuffs. Rubbing her arms, she sat back down, conscious of feeling strangely calm even as he watched her every movement. She hadn't been in a police station in a few years, but it already felt familiar. Even the smell was the same, a mix of sweat and cigarette smoke. Old feelings began to resurface, a mix of disgust and dread that made her skin crawl. She took a breath, steeling herself.

A woman came in, glanced at Nicky, then sat down at the desk directly in front of her. She was short, somewhere in her forties—at least a decade older than the guy. The man introduced her as Anna Ackerman, himself as Cullen Fraser. They were detectives. He didn't say partners, but it seemed a given.

Ackerman's desk was messy. She had to sift through some files to find the one she was looking for. His was tidy, two piles of paper neatly stacked, a laptop computer, a picture in a frame she couldn't see.

Fraser leaned against the front of Ackerman's desk—to the side so he didn't block Ackerman—just a couple of feet away, and looked down at Nicky. If his aim was to be intimidating, he'd have to try harder.

The woman said, "Let's start with your name, and age."

Nicky crossed her arms, happy to focus her attention on Ackerman. "Nicole Bosko. Twenty-five."

Ackerman wrote that down on a notepad in front of her. "You're originally from Stephenville, just north of Riverton?"

Nicky nodded. "That's correct."

"You work at Stevens Youth Shelter?" She started writing something.

Something strange was going on, as if this weren't about Michelle at all, but about herself. "You seem to know that already," she said cautiously.

Fraser's face hardened. "Yes or no will be fine."

Somewhere along the line he'd rolled up his shirt sleeves. Veins popped on his ripped arms and the room seemed way too small for that much sweaty manliness. She could practically smell the testosterone.

She looked at Ackerman. "Yes."

The questions continued like this for several minutes. They asked her when she'd moved to Riverton, what courses she was taking at college. They dropped hints that they knew about her youth record but made no mention of Michelle. She drummed her fingers on the arm of the chair, tried to think of why they would be harassing her, but came up short. She'd been a good girl. In detective shows, the cops often used clever tactics to interview suspects but she couldn't figure this out. If it wasn't about Michelle, what was it? In another minute, she would ask for a phone call. The shelter had to know Michelle was on her own.

Five minutes later, just as Nicky decided it had to be a strange hoax, Fraser said, "Who was the girl?"

Nicky shifted. Here it comes. "Just a kid I met on the street."

He cocked an eyebrow. "Why'd she take off?"

Shrugging, she gave her best version of nonchalant. "She's shy."

"Do you realize it's an offence to run from the cops?"

"I didn't realize you were a cop."

Icy eyes narrowing, Fraser shook his head slowly in disbelief. He knew she was lying—and he knew she knew he knew—but she didn't care. Now didn't seem a good time to disclose her motto: Rules were made to be broken.

Ackerman said, "Tell me about your family."

She stiffened, sat forward. "Are they okay? Was there an accident?"

The woman gave a small smile. "They're fine. We just have some routine questions."

She sat back, swallowed. Her patience wearing thin, she blew out a breath. "I have a father, James, and a sister. Her name is Karina. She's five years older."

The man watched her closely but seemed content to let the woman ask the questions. Ackerman opened a file on the desk in front of her. "Your father is a doctor?"

"That's correct. He's a perinatologist. That's—"

"A specialty for high-risk pregnancies," Fraser cut in before she could explain. He leaned over, looked at a newspaper clipping. "I see your sister is a nurse. And a concert pianist. Very accomplished."

You bet, Sherlock. She nodded at the clipping. "That's probably about her latest recording, one of the Bach concertos." The local paper went nuts about her sister. They couldn't resist her fresh-faced good looks. In Riverton, Karina was a superstar. Nicky wasn't any kind of star. A chronic underachiever is what her father had always called her, not realizing that it would only make her more rebellious.

He brushed a stray strand of hair out of his eyes, then crossed his arms over his big chest again. Something animalistic about him made a little shiver shoot through her. He should find a way to neuter some of that sexiness.

He said, "And your mother?"

She froze. He waited, eyebrows raised. "What about my mother?" Her voice sounded flat and emotionless even to herself.

Ackerman read from a file. "You last saw your mother, Lisa Bosko, when you were five?"

Managing a nod, she kept her eyes on Ackerman, acutely aware that Fraser watched her like a hawk watched its prey. She took a steadying breath, then another, and tried to think where this was headed. When they didn't say anything else, she said, "There isn't much to tell. She took off and I haven't seen her since."

He raised an eyebrow and those sharp eyes were on her. "What do you mean, 'took off'?"

Gripping the chair, she inhaled deeply. What possible justification could they have for asking her these questions? "She walked out of the house one day and we never saw her again. That's what I mean by 'took off.'" She glared at him, her dislike growing by the minute.

"Did you see her leave?" This question came from Ackerman.

"No. I came home from school one day and she was gone." Her fingernails dug into the upholstered arms of the chair. She's most likely living quite happily somewhere with another family, unless she'd decided to ditch them, too. "Why are you asking me this?" she asked Ackerman, who was the good cop to Fraser's bad, it seemed.

"We'll get to that," she said.

Nicky sat forward, a sour taste in her mouth. An explanation came to her. "Have you found her? Is that it? She wants to meet me?" When they didn't respond, she shook her head. "Not going to happen."

The cops exchanged a look but Nicky wasn't about to try to explain herself. What they thought of her was no concern.

Ackerman said, "So you haven't seen her in twenty years?"

"Correct. Apparently I was too much to handle." The words got out before she could catch them.

Ackerman nodded. "We've read a transcript of an interview conducted at the time with your father. There was apparently some suggestion you had some behavioral problems that caused difficulty at home."

She swallowed hard, shot the woman a hard look. "Apparently so. I don't remember it myself. I suppose I was too busy causing those problems." A bitter tang rose in her mouth. "Why are you asking this? Did I commit some crime when I was five that you're interested in?"

Ackerman ignored the question. "Were you interviewed?"

"Again. I don't remember. I was five."

Fraser's jaw hardened even more. "You're not five now. Have you ever tried to find your mother?" His tone was accusatory.

"Why would I?" They obviously didn't get it. Her mother clearly didn't want anything to do with her or her father and sister. "You should be talking to my father."

"That's going to be a bit of a challenge. Your father and sister have left the country."

"Left the country?"

He raised skeptical eyebrows. "You didn't know?" When she didn't say anything, he continued, "They're in Haiti, in a remote area on a relief mission. We've been trying to reach them, but the cell phone service is sketchy. They're not due back for another week."

She shrugged. That they hadn't informed her was no surprise. "I can't help you there."

Neither of them seemed to believe her, which was natural enough if you weren't familiar with how her family worked. Her father and sister were tight, always had been, even before her mother left. After her mother disappeared, Nicky became the fifth wheel.

But that was the past. She was over it. Even the resentment—no, hatred—she'd felt toward her mother had softened through the years to a casual indifference. She wasn't going to explain any of this to them. How somewhere along the line, somewhere between the ages of five and fifteen, she'd realized that her mother had moved on. And Nicky, a rebel but not a masochist, had done the same. Now, her mother's face was a blur and few memories remained of her early childhood. It helped that her father hadn't let them so much as mention her mother's name.

But she was a big girl now. She could look after herself. And she didn't have to answer any questions about her mother. She picked up her shoulder bag. "I'm not under arrest, am I? I'm free to go at any time?"

The woman said, "There's one more thing we want to ask you about before you go." She searched through the folders on her desk, found the one she was looking for and opened it. "Why did you take a DNA test?"

* * *

Nicole Bosko was gorgeous. Tall and slim, with a perfect oval face framed by long brown hair. Big brown eyes and high cheekbones that hinted at Slavic ancestry. It was an easy beauty, the kind that might have been spoiled by too much makeup, but she wore little or maybe even none and seemed unaware of the effect of her looks.

Or maybe she was very much aware. Cullen Fraser had no idea.

Good looks aside, one thing he could say for certain: she was a piece of work. Evasive, belligerent. A liar. And altogether too calm for someone being questioned by the police. He couldn't shake the feeling she was playing with them. The barely perceptible smile of contempt playing on her full lips didn't help.

Cullen nailed her with a stare. "You heard the question? Why did you take a DNA test?" His voice remained calm only with a conscious effort.

Ignoring him, she glanced at Anna, her brows knitted in confusion. "DNA test?"

Scowling, he grabbed a file from the desk and waved it in front of her. "The DNA test you took under the name of Nola Deveau." He slammed it down on the desk, stood up, and hovered over her. "You're not going to deny that, too, are you?"

Pink splotches on her cheeks replaced the sardonic smile. "How do you know about that?"

He clenched his fist, pleased they had finally managed to prick a hole in that tough shell. "I'd say that is the least of your worries."

"It's not against the law, is it, to have your DNA mapped? People do it all the time to test for diseases."

"Just answer the question: why did you take it?" He was aware only when he finished speaking his voice had risen. Anna shot him a warning look. Pressing his lips together, he took some deep breaths, walked over to the metal cabinet, and leaned against it.

Anna said, "The sooner you answer our questions, the sooner you'll get out of here. Why did you take the test? What were you looking for?"

Bosko squeezed her eyes shut for a moment, opened them.

They were dark, the color of deep mahogany, and spaced wide apart. Too wide apart, but they were balanced by a strong chin, and something about them suggested a sharp intelligence.

She said, her tone cold, "I took a genetics course last spring. A couple of us in the class decided to do it. I certainly didn't have any criminal intent."

Anna said, "So why did you use an assumed name?"

"Because I didn't feel comfortable giving a private company access to my genetic information. And I don't like the fact that you now have it." Her eyes had gone cold to match her tone. "How did you find out it was me?"

He walked over to the desk, leaned against it, wanting to be in her face. "You weren't that clever about it. You used the shelter address, so that narrowed it down fairly quickly."

The pink spots on her face turned red. "That doesn't explain why you have it. I haven't left my DNA at any crime scene, as far as I'm aware."

Cullen watched her closely. It was a good bet she'd had her DNA tested in hopes of tracking down her mother. Why not just admit it? Unless she was in some other kind of trouble. Which was more than possible, given her record.

He said, "You still haven't told us why you ran. If you've gotten yourself into some little thing, just tell us. We're not interested."

A look of vulnerability flashed in her eyes then quickly disappeared. "It would help if you would tell me what exactly you *are* interested in."

He exchanged a glance with Anna, who stood up. She addressed Bosko, "Would you like some coffee?" When Bosko nodded, Anna motioned for him to follow her.

In the kitchen, Anna filled three mugs with coffee, then turned to him, hands on her hips. "This is going nowhere. We're wasting time."

"She's lying."

She raised her eyebrows in answer.

He said, "Why'd she run, then?"

She gave him a soft punch in the shoulder. "Maybe she just didn't like the looks of you."

He frowned. "I don't give a shit whether she likes me or not."

"She sure has figured out how to push your buttons."

Rolling his eyes, he decided to ignore the comment. It seemed too close to the truth. "What if she had something to do with her mother's disappearance? It's obvious she doesn't give a shit about her mother. And it sounded like she was a hell-raiser as a kid."

"You think she was an evil five-year-old who plotted to get rid of her mother? Why? So she could have her daddy all to herself?"

He took a sip of coffee, grimaced at the bitter taste. "Maybe she saw something. Maybe she's protecting someone. It could be her father. It's obvious she's hiding something. We have to find out what that is."

Anna considered this for a moment, then nodded. "A few more questions, then we have to tell her." She grabbed his arm as he was about to walk away. "I'm sorry about Marlee."

His breath caught. "I suppose that's all over the squad

room." His girlfriend of three years, a television news reporter, had told him two days ago she was leaving him for another cop. They had talked about getting married, settling down. Now he was left wondering how long she'd been seeing the other cop behind his back. "Fuck it," he said.

When they got back to the room, he handed Bosko a mug. She brushed a strand of hair behind her ear, then took a sip.

Anna said, "Sorry, it's pretty foul."

Bosko made no reaction. She waited until Anna had sat down, then said, "Why don't you just tell me what this is about? Has my mother gone missing again? Is her new family looking for her?"

He clenched his fists at her scornful tone. Man, this woman was a piece of work.

She was about to take another sip of coffee, but must have thought better of it because she leaned forward and set the mug on the desk in front of her. "Please be careful about approaching my father. He had a heart attack last year. He shouldn't be bothered about this."

Anna shot Cullen a look, then said, "What do you remember about the day she left?"

"There we go again. Asking questions you already have the answers for."

There was no emotion in her expression. Either she didn't feel any or she did a damn good job of suppressing it. He was about to say something but held back. She seemed to want to piss him off. As if not giving a shit about her mother wasn't already accomplishing that goal.

When they both just gave her blank looks, she said, "I came

home from school and she wasn't there. It was two decades ago. That's all I remember."

He said, "How can you not remember more?

She shrugged. "It may seem hard to believe, but if you don't think about something, it's easy to forget."

He nodded. The explanation made sense. "Did you see her leave?"

"No, I did not." She spoke slowly, emphasizing her words. "But everybody knew she wanted to leave."

"Why do you say that?"

"There was a note. Don't you have it?"

She played with a thin gold necklace around her neck, then her hand dropped to her lap. Her breasts, firm and round, molded to the thin fabric of her T-shirt. Swallowing hard, he looked away.

Anna said, "We don't have all the case files yet, although we've seen a reference to a note she apparently left."

"There's no mystery. She didn't want to stay." She bit her lip, sighed. "It may be hard for you to believe, but I've spent a couple of decades trying not to think about Lisa Bosko. I have no idea where she went or where she is now." She glanced at her watch.

He said, "Did you find out anything interesting? In the DNA?"

"Most of it was useless, if you must know. I don't have any risk factors for inherited diseases. My chances of having a heart attack are slightly higher. And apparently I have a gene that makes me rebellious, although they couldn't pinpoint the location."

Not missing a beat, he said, "It's on the long arm of chromosome seven, right next to the one for being uncooperative."

She shot him a mock-sweet smile. "I see you've read the report."

Ignoring the quip, he said, "Did you check for relatives?"

She cocked an eyebrow at him. "There was nobody close." She looked at her watch again, then at Anna. "I have to go to work. I will contact a lawyer to ensure information about my DNA is kept private."

His partner said, "We have no use for it. It will be deleted; you can be sure of that." Anna stood up. "We want to show you something."

Bosko shot her a withering look and stood up. "I really don't care what you have got to show me."

He walked to the tall metal cabinet, opened the door. On the top shelf was a clay sculpture of a woman's head. It looked so much like Bosko—the oval face, high cheekbones, wide-set eyes, small mouth—it was as if she'd posed for it. A few things were off, the face too fleshy, the nose too short. But a chill ran down his spine at seeing it again.

At the door, Bosko reached for the handle, then glanced back. For a split second, her expression didn't change, then she raised a hand to her mouth and the color drained from her face. She looked from his face to Anna's, then walked slowly as if in a trance and stood in front of the cabinet. One shaky hand reached out to touch the sculpture but drew back.

Looking at him, her lips moved, but it was a moment before words emerged. "Why do you have a bust of me?"

He said, "You should sit down."

"I don't want to sit down. Tell me." The words came out ragged, barely audible.

He said, "It's a facial reconstruction, but it's not you."

"Who is it?" Realization dawning, she covered her mouth again. Shock had darkened her eyes to a coal black.

"It's your mother."

Acknowledgments

A big thanks to my family and friends for their encouragement and support. And to my editor, Dana Hamilton of Hachette Book Group, for taking me on and being such a great person to work with.

About the Author

An award-winning writer of romantic suspense, Alex Kingwell is a former newspaper reporter, columnist, and editor, who much prefers spending her days making stories up. When she's not writing, or stuck with her head in a book, Alex can be found running with her dog, obsessing over tribal textiles, or watching offbeat movies with her husband (not necessarily in that order). She lives on the Canadian Prairies.

Learn more at:

Twitter: @AlexKingwell

Web: AlexKingwell.com

9 781455 565313